"You have a problem, I have a solution. One that isn't marry me and live unhappily ever after."

Flora gave a tense nod and thought, *I'm probably going to regret this.* "I'm listening."

"I suggest you and Jamie come back to Italy with me. Think of it as a holiday."

"To Italy! What would that solve? Anyway," she said, shaking her head from side to side, "I'm not going anywhere with you."

Ivo dug a hand into his pocket, catching the velvet pouch that held the ring in his fingers. "How about you hear me out?"

She responded to the sardonic request with a slow, reluctant nod of her head.

"Come back to Italy with me as my fiancée."

Kim Lawrence lives on a farm in Anglesey with her university-lecturer husband, assorted pets who arrived as strays and never left, and sometimes one or both of her boomerang sons. When she's not writing, she loves to be outdoors gardening or walking on one of the beaches for which the island is famous—along with being the place where Prince William and Catherine made their first home!

Books by Kim Lawrence

Harlequin Presents

Santiago's Command
The Petrelli Heir
Captivated by Her Innocence
One Night with Morelli
Surrendering to the Italian's Command
A Ring to Secure His Crown
The Greek's Ultimate Conquest
A Cinderella for the Desert King

One Night With Consequences

A Secret Until Now
Her Nine-Month Confession

Wedlocked!

One Night to Wedding Vows

Seven Sexy Sins

The Sins of Sebastian Rey-Defoe

Visit the Author Profile page
at Harlequin.com for more titles.

Kim Lawrence

A WEDDING AT THE
ITALIAN'S DEMAND

H HARLEQUIN PRESENTS®

Recycling programs
for this product may
not exist in your area.

ISBN-13: 978-1-335-47815-3

A Wedding at the Italian's Demand

First North American publication 2019

Copyright © 2019 by Kim Lawrence

Printed in U.S.A.

A WEDDING AT THE ITALIAN'S DEMAND

CHAPTER ONE

THE LIGHT IN the wide corridor Ivo Greco walked along was muted, but the priceless tapestries that lined the stone walls provided their own glowing illumination as he moved towards the massive double doors of etched glass at the far end. The doors had to stay closed to maintain the carefully controlled humidity and light to preserve the priceless antiques.

They provided a light-at-the-end-of-the-tunnel effect, but it was an illusion. Ivo was *not* expecting any version of a heavenly vision on the other side because the doors led to his grandfather's private apartments, to which Ivo had been summoned.

His grandfather had actually sent for him forty-eight hours ago, and people did not keep Salvatore Greco waiting!

While Salvatore was on the record as saying he respected people who stood up to him, the reality was that Salvatore, a man who possessed vast wealth and enormous power, also possessed a very fragile ego.

As an eight-year-old, when Salvatore had taken over the guardianship of him and his brother, Ivo had not understood about egos, but he had quickly realised that it was easy to make his grandfather angry.

It had actually been the day before his eighth birthday when Ivo's father had decided he could no longer live without his late wife. Ivo had found his father's body and his grandfather had found Ivo.

Amid the horror of that day Ivo remembered the strength in his grandfather's arms, the sanctuary they had afforded as he had picked Ivo up and taken him away from the scene that had lived on for years in his childish nightmares.

Even as a young boy Ivo had understood that he owed his grandfather a debt impossible to repay, and this knowledge did not disappear when he realised his grandfather was no guardian angel or superhero but a hard, ruthless man, not always fair and almost impossible to please.

But the fact remained that, no matter what he did, Salvatore was the one who had carried Ivo out of his hell. The debt remained, as did the gratitude burnt deep into his soul by the character-changing events of that day. Ivo had long ago stopped trying to please, even though he knew better than most that the old man hated to be thwarted and just how viciously he could react to any perceived insult, real or imagined. A very good reason why the people that surrounded Salvatore rarely disagreed with him, at least to his face.

Ivo was sanguine about the reception he was likely to receive, more bothered about the necessity of postponing a meeting than the tirade of abuse and invective inevitably waiting for him.

A nerve twitched along his hard jawline as, unbidden, a memory floated into his head; he had not always been so philosophical.

It had taken his brother several minutes to coax him out of his hiding place in one of the warren of attics in the *palazzo*. He couldn't remember what he had done to outrage his grandparent but he remembered not believing his brother when he had said, 'Never show him you're afraid, then one day you won't be.'

Ivo pushed the memory away, his symmetrical features hardening; the past was gone.

In his view there were few things more pathetic than people who clung onto memories until they became defined by their past. He saw them everywhere, from the people who became fixated on missed opportunities, old hurts and injustices, to the guy who constantly relived his early successes on the sports field, as if lifting a trophy at twenty defined him. All were so consumed with the past that they missed the opportunities that the future offered.

Ivo's sights were always fixed ahead, though at that moment it was something in the periphery of his vision that caught his attention.

The suited servant, a new face to Ivo, who had shadowed him since he'd entered the building, almost collided with him as Ivo came to an unscheduled halt. Ivo let the man's apologies slide off him as, head tilted back, he moved backwards to get the full effect of the glowing Byzantine image on the wall, again nearly falling over the man behind who delivered another flustered apology.

'New?'

'I'm not sure, sir.'

The response was perfectly polite but under the surface Ivo could almost feel the anxiety rolling off the man and, after one last glance at the wall, he took pity on him. Turning away, he caught sight of a look of relief on the man's face; it was that look and not his own anxiety that made him quicken his leisurely pace.

Ivo's personal spaces were minimalist and uncluttered—functional could still be pleasing to the eye or at least his eyes—but he appreciated beauty and artistic talent in many forms. He would have liked to study this testament to the skill of long-dead artisans for longer. The irony, of course, was that his grandfather would not appreciate the beauty.

Salvatore was a famed collector of many rare and precious objects—jade, art, porcelain—but for him it was all about the acquisition. For Salvatore, the pleasure came from possessing what someone else wanted. He might forget the history of an artwork or the name of an artist, but he had a flawless recall of the price he'd paid for any item and the identity of the collectors he outbid.

Once through the doors and into a brighter corridor, thanks to massive windows that revealed breath catching views of the Tyrrhenian Sea that glittered turquoise in the Tuscan morning sun, Ivo turned to his shadow.

'I think I know my way from here.'

The man hesitated; clearly Ivo's words clashed with his instructions. He began to bluster but his protests trailed away as Ivo's dark level stare held his, and after a moment he tipped his head and faded away. Ivo's grandfather's private apartments were situated in one of the older parts of the building, taking up all of one of the iconic twelfth-century square towers built by an ancestor. The massive metal banded door to the study was open and Ivo walked straight in. He was prepared; even so he experienced a moment's disorientation as he stepped over the threshold, feeling as if he'd stepped through some time portal or onto the set of a futuristic film. He almost reached for the designer shades tucked into the pocket of his suit jacket, the antiseptic white and chrome was that dazzling.

Five years earlier his grandfather had ripped out the antique panelling along with the books that had once lined the walls, and the decor was now sleek and modern. *Efficient,* as his grandfather had said as they'd watched the monitors being mounted on the wall, the only thing left from the past the antique desk that dominated the room.

A half-smile flickered across Ivo's wide sensual mouth as he recalled the occasion he had casually admitted that he missed the old room, inviting further scorn when he had added he actually *liked* the smell of musty old books. This had apparently confirmed his grandfather's suspicion that Ivo was a sentimental fool.

Ivo had accepted the insult with a careless shrug of his wide shoulders, aware that if Salvatore had believed either of these things he would not have given him control of the IT and Communications division of Greco Industries, although *given* was perhaps the wrong word. When the grand gesture was made his grandfather had not anticipated the role would have any permanence.

His gratitude at the time had been genuine even though Ivo had known that it had been intended as a wing-clipping exercise—the unspoken but universally acknowledged expectation had been that the young upstart would fail; indeed he was *meant* to fail, publicly.

But Ivo had defied those expectations, denying his grandfather the opportunity to ride to the rescue. A source of frustration to a man who liked to be in control.

And *so far*, Ivo had been allowed a free hand.

Was that about to change?

He was not given to paranoia but neither was Ivo a believer in coincidence, and the timing of this peremptory summons, coinciding as it did with the ink drying on the new global merger he had negotiated, had raised a few warning bells. Was it significant that this merger would mean the IT division was no longer the poor relation of Greco Industries but able to challenge the leisure, property and construction arms of the company, and even make the jewel in the crown, Greco's media division, look over their shoulder?

So far Salvatore had been content to bask in the reflected glory of his grandson's success but maybe that was no longer enough. Was he about to announce he wanted to be more hands on?

Ivo approached the possibility with more curiosity than trepidation. Considering the fact Salvatore was a control freak, this scenario had always been a possibility and Ivo had already decided that, rather than surrender his control, or even share it, he would walk away.

Just looking for an excuse, Ivo?

His dark brows twitching into a frown that drew them into a straight line above his masterful nose, he ignored the sly voice in his head as he cleared his throat.

In reality he knew he would never walk away from his duty, any more than his grandfather had walked away from him. Ivo was not his father, or his brother.

'Morning, Grandfather.'

Close to eighty, Salvatore Greco remained an imposing figure. There was nothing fragile or infirm about his upright stance, but as he turned to face his grandson Ivo found himself thinking, for the first time in his life, that his grandfather was old.

Maybe it was the morning light shining directly on the older man's face as he turned, revealing the depth of the lines that grooved his forehead and etched deep the furrows carved from his nose to the downward-turning corners of his thin mouth.

The line of silent speculation vanished the moment the older man began to speak, as did pretty much every other thought. There was definitely no hint of age or softness in his voice as he delivered his announcement.

'Your brother is dead.' He took his seat in the high-backed chair behind the massive antique desk that still dominated the otherwise minimally furnished white room, pausing only to straighten the line of meticulously sharpened pencils before he continued to speak.

Ivo didn't notice a tremor in his grandfather's voice as he stared blindly ahead, and the words just rolled over him in a meaningless jumble until one sentence made itself heard above the loud static hum in his head.

'I will need you to take care of this personally, you understand?'

Ivo fought his way through the swirl of churning emotions that made their physical presence known in the fog in his head and the constricting band that felt like steel around his chest before he spoke.

'The funeral?' It still didn't seem possible— would it ever? Bruno—nine years his senior...what did that make him? Thirty-eight? How did anyone die at thirty-eight?

Outrage at the thought elicited a mind-calming burst of rage followed swiftly by denial. It had to be a mistake. Yes, that was it, some awful mistake. If his brother was dead, he'd know.

His grandfather's eyes narrowed fractionally as his lips compressed in faint irritation at the interruption.

'Their funeral was last month, I believe.'

The words ricocheted around in Ivo's head. He needed to sit down. His fingers clenched his knuckles white against the leather armrest...he *was* sitting down. He had been walking around functioning as normal for weeks while his brother was dead. How could he not have known, not have *felt* something? He tipped his head in a sharp motion of denial and cut across his grandfather, who was speaking again.

'Last month?'

His grandfather looked at him without speaking before he reached for the stopper on the crystal decanter that sat on the desk and glugged some of the amber liquid into one of the glasses that sat beside it on the silver tray.

The full glass scraped on the desk as he pushed it towards his grandson.

Ivo shook his head, not mistaking the action for empathy; he had accepted years ago that his grandparent was incapable of that. Emotional responses were, in Salvatore's eyes, weaknesses to be studied and exploited. It was not coincidental that Ivo was famed for his unreadable expression. What had begun as a self-protective device was now second nature.

'You said *their*?' Ivo's brain was starting to function, but he was not sure if that could be classed as a good thing. The sense of loss had a physical presence; he could feel it at a cellular level in a way he'd sworn never to feel anything again. As he'd coped alone after Bruno's desertion, the realisation that he could not count on anyone else had required he closed off the part of himself that made him vulnerable to such painful feelings. And now, the unfamiliar dormant feelings had exploded into painful life, blurring his normally sharp-edged wits.

'The woman was with him.'

'His *wife*.' Ivo emphasised the word as an image flashed into his head, probably not even accurate.

He'd only met the woman his brother had walked away from his own family for once, and that had been fourteen years ago. Her eyes probably hadn't been *that* blue, but the memory of that vivid colour had stayed with him even after the resentment towards Samantha Henderson had faded. Samantha was, after all, responsible for robbing Ivo of the big brother he had worshipped and the future he had dreamt of.

Not immediately, Bruno was coming to get him, he had promised, tears on his cheeks as he, Ivo, had begged his brother not to leave. How long had it taken him to realise that Bruno was never coming back?

Fool, mocked the derisive voice in his head as he thought of his younger self waiting, believing. Bruno had said what Ivo had wanted to hear. In truth, he'd never intended coming back for him; he had deserted him.

The people in Ivo's life had a habit of doing that: first his father, then Bruno. A person who invited that sort of pain and disillusion had to be a fool, and Ivo was no fool.

In a world obsessed with pairing people off, he had learnt that, far from being a deficiency, being alone was a strength. He never intended to be in a position where someone else had the power to inflict that sort of pain. He was not looking for love; love exaggerated men's weaknesses, left a man less than whole.

To this point it hadn't been difficult to avoid the infection of *love*, any more difficult than walking away from sexual encounters. The compartments in his life remained unpolluted by love, but *loyalty* was another thing.

His grandfather never demanded love but he did demand loyalty and Ivo considered he had earned it. The only person who had ever been there for him was Salvatore; a man who didn't pretend to be something he wasn't. The old man was a devil, but he didn't hide behind a saint's mask.

Bruno had been his favourite grandson.

His heir.

Ivo, who'd worshipped his brother, had been fine with that.

There had always been an expectation that Ivo would one day rebel, and, growing up, his occasional failures, while not going unpunished, were almost *expected*. It was whispered that he was like his father; that he had inherited the same weakness.

Ivo had heard the whispers, gritted his teeth and determined that he would prove them all wrong. It was not news to him that his father was weak, because only a weak man would take his own life and leave two motherless sons behind because he couldn't live without the woman he loved.

His mother must have been special, Bruno always said she was, but Ivo didn't really remember his mother at all. He didn't allow himself to remember his father; instead he despised him.

For his brother it had always been different— he was the golden boy. Not easy—the bar had been set high for the heir to his grandfather's empire and failure was not tolerated, and he'd lived up to expectations, which was perhaps why, when he'd finally challenged Salvatore, the consequences had been so extreme.

Salvatore had already had a bride picked out for his heir. It would be a profitable union, as the woman was the only child and heir of a man almost as wealthy as the Grecos and with an equally proud lineage, which for his grandfather was almost as important. He was fond of speaking of bloodlines and pointing out the proof that the Grecos, who could trace their bloodlines back centuries, were among the elite of Europe.

Ivo had been fifteen when his brother had walked away to be with the woman he loved. He'd finally realised when the brother he idolised had not returned for him that the whispers had been wrong all along. *Ivo* hadn't been the one who had inherited their father's weakness; Bruno was the one that couldn't live without the woman he loved.

But Bruno could live without honour, and his little brother.

His older brother had betrayed him but, even so, Bruno had been *living* out there somewhere, some place cold and bleak, a Scottish island, but now he wasn't.

It didn't seem possible.

'Nobody informed you?' He pressed a finger to the groove between his dark brows, struggling to make sense of what he was hearing.

His grandfather's bushy brows lifted. 'Obviously I was informed, by your brother's solicitor. Oh, and the woman's sister sent a letter, handwritten,' he added with a contemptuous snort. 'Barely legible.'

Ivo shook his head and felt anger separate itself out from the multi-layered raw emotions churning in his belly. Tangled as they were with the irrational guilt he refused to acknowledge, the physical effort of keeping the toxic mixture in check sent fine tremors through his lean body.

'You knew?' A muscle along his jaw clenched and quivered as the old man simply shrugged in confirmation, feeding the flame of fury inside him. He could feel it building. None of his feelings showed on his face but there was ice in his voice when he pressed his point. 'And you did not see fit to share that information with me, until now?'

There was the slightest edge of defiance in Salvatore's voice as he met his grandson's eyes and bit out, 'What would have been the point, Bruno?'

The muscles along Ivo's jawline quivered. His grandfather seemed unaware of what he had called him, his heavy eyelids lowered over dark flame-lit eyes.

'It did not occur to you that I might want to go to the funeral?' *Would he have...?* Well, he'd never know now, he concluded with bitter irony.

'No, it didn't. You had your *closure* all those years ago when he stopped being your brother, and...' Eyes that held no expression flickered as he scanned his grandson's face. 'You're not a hypocrite.' He arched a brow, his lip curling in mild mocking contempt as he threw out the challenge. 'Are you?'

Ivo's head came up slowly, his almond-shaped dark eyes resting without expression on his grandfather's face. The surge of colour that had highlighted the slashing curves of his razor-edged cheekbones had receded. The normal vibrant olive glow had been overwhelmed by a waxy pallor that gave his features the sepia cast of an old photo; his features were utterly still. Only the nerve spasmodically clenching to the right of his clamped bloodless lips a sign of life.

He shook his head in an attitude of someone expecting to wake up. 'Bruno contacted me eighteen months ago. He wanted to meet up.' Ivo, staring blankly into middle distance, did not see the look of anger that crossed his grandfather's face. He was too consumed with the guilt clawing low in his belly.

'You met up with him?'

Ivo turned his head, the bleakness in his eyes profound. If the love he'd felt for his brother really had died when he hadn't come back, should he be feeling this sort of pain now?

Pushing the question away, he took a deep breath and squared his shoulders. A man took responsibility for his actions. 'No, I didn't.'

A decision that he might never forgive himself for now. His brother had reached out and he had rejected him, and why? Because he had carried the anger and resentment of a youth into adulthood, because he wanted to punish Bruno?

Self-contempt quivered queasily in his belly, guilt and regret adding to the toxic sensation. The fact was he could have forgiven the desertion but he could never have forgiven the lie that had kept hope alive.

'I thought he'd given up on that,' the old man mused, dragging a hand over the grey stubble on his chin.

'Given up?'

'Bruno kept away after I took out the injunction,

but the letters carried on for... Well, they stopped too...' Salvatore frowned. 'When was that...? No matter, they stopped after the lawyers made it clear that if he contacted you again I'd disinherit the pair of you and it would be *his* responsibility.'

A hand pressed against the dull throb in his head as Ivo struggled to make sense of what he was hearing. 'He came back for me?'

Salvatore snorted. 'Wanted guardianship, would you believe it?'

His expression invited Ivo to share his contempt at the idea, but Ivo was in no condition to share anything. Bruno *hadn't* lied, he hadn't deserted him.

'He came back.'

Salvatore gave an impatient click of his fingers. 'As if any court would have granted him access with his conviction.'

'Conviction?'

'I don't suppose you would know but your brother dabbled a bit. He fell in with a bad crowd at school and was caught with a small amount...easy enough to brush under the carpet but the record remained.'

'Drugs? Bruno?' No inkling of this youthful scandal had ever reached Ivo's ears; how much else had he been protected from?

He had given up on his brother but his brother had never given up on him! The discovery left a bittersweet taste in his mouth.

Salvatore's comments suggested that Bruno had not just come back, he had fought, reaching out again, but this time Ivo was the one who had walked away! Ivo sat there as the guilt closed in on him, wrapping its wire tendrils around him like a cage.

He had barely begun to process this reversal of everything he had believed when his grandfather landed another shock.

'The child—'

Ivo's head whipped around. 'What child?'

'Your brother had a son, a baby, he's...' He stabbed the air in an impatient gesture. 'It doesn't matter what they've called him... This is why I need you to go to Scotland, to the Isle of Skye—presumably you know that's where your brother has been living in some shack...probably no electricity and running water. I want you to fetch back the child. He belongs here with us—the father may have been a fool and his mother...' With a curl of his lip he dismissed Samantha. 'But the child is a Greco—he has a heritage.'

'How...?' Ivo's heavy lids half lowered as he swallowed to alleviate the emotional constriction in his throat. 'How did they die?' he finally managed to push out harshly.

'A climbing accident, they were roped together apparently. A witness at the inquest said they heard him begging her to cut the line, but she didn't—' For the first time Ivo imagined he heard emotion in his grandfather's voice as he added harshly, 'Ivo always had a reckless streak.' His grandfather's eyes drifted closed.

'*Bruno* always loved the mountains,' Ivo said softly. The gentle emphasis he placed on his brother's name seemed to pass over his grandfather's head.

He opened his eyes. 'That's what I just said! And look where it led…' he intoned bitterly. 'If he hadn't climbed he'd never have met that girl… A potter, living in a hovel.'

A slight exaggeration but Samantha had seemed a million miles from the perfectly groomed models and society women his brother had previously dated.

Love at first sight, Bruno had said.

As if he'd had no choice in the matter! Ivo hadn't believed that then or now. It was the excuse of a weak man, the man he had no intention of ever being.

There was *always* a choice.

Suddenly the mantra he lived his life by had less conviction.

'I have spoken to the lawyers but there is no way to break the will.'

'So there's a will—what does it say?' Ivo struggled to express interest he did not feel. All he could think about was Bruno and the fact that he had not betrayed him out of choice. Bruno had fought for him, admittedly against stacked odds, but he had fought nonetheless.

'Not relevant.'

It struck Ivo as very relevant but he said nothing. He was thinking about the son that Bruno had left behind; the child he could not desert. He had turned his back on his brother but he wouldn't turn his back on his nephew!

'They were young, the young never expect to die, and this Henderson woman…the sister…'

Ivo hadn't known there was a sister, but then why should he? 'Does she have a name?'

'Something Scottish… Fiona or, no, Flora, I think.'

'And she is the child's legal guardian?' Ivo found himself clinging to the knowledge that Bruno had a son; that a part of him lived on. Perhaps one day it would be a comfort, one day when the pain of loss was not so raw and his sense of guilt not so corrosive. What he needed to focus on now was not the guilt, but the fatherless child. *It's not about you, Ivo,* he reminded himself with a humourless half-smile.

His grandfather brought his fist down onto the desk top with a force that made the wood vibrate and drew a wince from his lips. 'It's ludicrous. She has… is…nothing!' he spat out contemptuously.

'You want to be a part of this child's life, maybe you should learn to say her name,' Ivo suggested mildly.

'I do not want her to be a *part* of this child's life. That family is responsible for me losing my grandson.'

That was certainly one way of looking at it and it was the one way Ivo had been encouraged to look at it. A way he still found he was reluctant to relinquish.

'Well, how is no compromise working for you so

far, Grandfather? Maybe you should be realistic and settle for what you can get.'

Salvatore's eyes narrowed. 'Is that the lesson in life you have learnt? *Settling?*' he snarled with withering contempt. 'I made her a perfectly reasonable offer—generous! She refused.'

'You offered to buy the child?' *Dio*, this got worse. His grandfather seemed to have lost the subtlety and cunning he was famed for. 'And you are surprised she refused?'

'Oh, I know what this is about. She's barren, can't have a baby of her own, so she's going to cling onto this one for dear life,' Salvatore brooded darkly. 'The letter she sent said it all…sentimental twaddle, inviting me to visit him there. I do not want *that* family in the child's life. They took him from…'

The old man's voice quivered; his eyes grew glassy and blank. The result of anger, or grief?

Or just the simple fact someone had thwarted him?

Whatever had put the quiver in his voice, it made the old man swallow and turn away. This rare visual evidence of vulnerability, the sudden appearance of frailty, struck deep, bringing the memory to the surface of the day when Salvatore had been strong. When he had rescued him from that room and the lifeless father Ivo had tried to awaken, even in his childish ignorance trying to push some of the pills that had spilled from one of the empty bottles past his father's cold lips, believing that the medicine would make him better. Not understanding until much later that the pills had been his father's weapon of choice.

Salvatore wanted to rescue this baby just as he had rescued Ivo. For Salvatore it was all about bloodlines!

Are you in any position to sneer? demanded the voice in Ivo's head. *For you, it's all about assuaging your guilt.*

His broad shoulders lifted in a shrug of acknowledgement; granted, neither motivation was particularly noble, but then the Grecos were not renowned for their nobility. His jaw stiffened—they were known for getting what they wanted, though.

Ivo stilled as the belated shocked recognition slid through him: he *wanted* to bring up this child, this part of Bruno who remained.

He gave them both a moment to recover before responding.

'Should I ask if this information is out in the public domain, or have you accessed this woman's private medical records?'

The older man responded to the dry question with a shrug and a sour look.

Ivo did not pursue it. He wasn't that bothered about the red lines Salvatore had gleefully crossed. The fact was that, guilt aside, and with a determination to make up for rejecting his brother, there was a part of him that could identify with his motivation.

It was not something he felt the need to apologise for. Ivo possessed an Italian's pride in his culture and language, a pride he knew his brother had shared, and thinking of Bruno's son missing out on this part of his heritage drew a dizzying number of intersecting red lines in his head. Ivo's loyalty to his name was unquestioning, it went cell deep, which was why his brother's defection had hurt so much. Bruno had rejected everything they had been brought up to respect.

But he had not rejected him; Bruno had come back for him.

The regret and guilt that he would never now have a chance to thank his brother were so powerful he could taste the metallic tang like blood on his tongue. He focused instead on the *wrongness* that the child that shared his DNA was out there somewhere, knowing nothing of his history.

He had a debt to repay to his brother, and he would. Giving his nephew the sort of upbringing he and Bruno had *not* had would be his atonement.

His grandfather seemed fully recovered, delivering an irritated scowl. 'We need leverage, but she's done nothing.'

'By that I presume you mean she has no skeletons?'

'There is the suggestion of an affair with some footballer, but he wasn't married at the time.'

'So what do you expect me to do, kidnap the child?'

'Yes,' would have been less shocking than the reply he received.

'I expect you to marry the woman, and bring the child home here. The lawyers say that will give you legal rights. It should make it simple to gain custody after the divorce.'

Ivo's moment of gobsmacked incredulity found release in laughter. When was the last time he'd laughed in his grandfather's presence? he wondered as he listened to the sound…rusty, as though he was out of practice. For some reason he could hear the sound of his brother's laughter in his head, too. When Bruno had left he had taken the laughter with him.

'Have you finished?' Salvatore asked, when the room fell silent.

There had been a time when the icy disdain had tied his stomach in knots of tension but that time was long gone. 'You appear to have given this some thought.'

'You trying to tell me you couldn't make her fall in love if you wanted to?'

'Thanks for the vote of confidence,' Ivo said drily as he got to his feet to place both hands on the desk before leaning forward and saying slowly, 'I don't want to.'

He had reached the door when his grandfather's words reached him.

'I'm dying and I want you to bring my great-grandson here. Do you really want your brother's son to be brought up by a stranger, never hearing his own language? Never having the advantages that being a Greco brings? Are you that selfish?'

Ivo turned slowly, his dark eyes sweeping his

grandfather's lined face. Yes, he *did* look old. 'Is that true?'

'You think I'd lie about such a thing?'

'Yes,' Ivo responded without hesitation.

The old man laughed and looked quite pleased, clearly taking the comment as a compliment. 'I would like to retain a little dignity in what is a very undignified process. I have no intention of boring you with the unpleasant details, but I am dying, and I want to see the boy. Will you do that for me?'

Ivo's chest lifted as he released the breath held in his chest. 'I make no promises,' he said, while making a promise to himself—there was no way in the world he would hand over a baby to Salvatore, but he would bring this child home and he would protect him from the full force of Salvatore's frequently toxic influence, just as Bruno had protected him.

His grandfather smiled. 'I knew you wouldn't let me down, Bruno.'

CHAPTER TWO

FLORA TIPTOED STEALTHILY down the stairs, wincing as the board beneath her feet creaked. She froze, balanced on one foot, only releasing the breath held in her chest in a sigh of shuddering relief when there was no sound of baby sobs from upstairs.

Her mum said her grandson was teething, but then she also said that Jamie was an *easy* baby.

After the past few weeks Flora was of the opinion that easy babies were fictional creatures much like elves, or unicorns, only they slept less.

Flora could *vaguely* remember what sleep was. She had begun to feel increasingly nostalgic for a time when her idea of a bad night was tossing and turning for half an hour before she drifted off.

Now she could sleep standing up; she *had* slept standing up!

Sami had made it look so easy. Flora's blue eyes filled with unshed tears and she blinked hard as she choked out her sister's name in a forlorn whisper. She was so focused on the image in her head of her smiling sister and the physical pain of loss that it took her a few moments to register the cold.

Very cold, cold she hadn't noticed upstairs, but then walking several miles up and down the cheerily furnished nursery wearing a groove in the carpet while jiggling the cranky baby and humming an irritating jingle advertising a deodorant—not a very appropriate lullaby but she couldn't get the darned thing out of her head—was one way to keep warm.

She shivered, and gathered the thick cardigan she had put on over her sweater tightly around her. Nepotism aside, she was proud of her very first project as a qualified architect. The conversion of the derelict stone steading her sister and brother-in-law had decided to convert into their home and business, a restaurant with rooms, had won her a mention, though no glittering prize, in a prestigious competition.

Heating and insulation had been a priority in the brief and normally it was warm and cosy, not to mention wildly ecologically efficient with its state-of-the-art heating system, triple glazing that muffled the sound of the storm outside, and a roof of solar panels, but tonight the cold draughts seemed to have discovered ways inside.

She didn't realise there was more involved than the storm raging outside and some uninsulated nooks and crannies until she brushed past one of the tall modernist column radiators and, instead of feeling comforting heat, her fingers made contact with metal that was stone cold.

She groaned and tried not to think of the missed boiler service she had deemed a reasonable economy, because everything seemed to be working fine and anyway it was state-of-the-art, didn't that mean something?

Easy with the clarity of hindsight to recognise a classic case of false economy.

She allowed herself a self-pitying sniff or three before squaring her slender shoulders. *Right, Flora, beat yourself up tomorrow and call the heating guy—right now stop whining and make the best of it.*

She considered her immediate options. Retreating to the small private living room, an oak-framed extension with incredible views over the water to the mainland, wasn't one because she'd not got around to lighting the wood burner in there earlier and, with the underfloor heating off and a wall of glass, it would be even colder than in here.

So maybe the best move was make a hot-water bottle, put the spare heaters in the nursery and climb into bed. It might only be eight-thirty but her body clock was so out of sync thanks to chronic sleep deprivation that it didn't really matter—yes, that was definitely a plan.

So, first things first, the heater in the nursery then make herself a hot-water bottle. Her thick wool socks made no sound on the stone floor of the reception-area-cum-lounge and informal bar space while there was a perceptible increase in the volume of the storm raging outside.

Her shiver this time was for anyone unlucky enough not to have several feet of solid stone between them and the elements. Continuing to switch off lights as she went—at least they still had electricity—she fished her mobile from the pocket of her snug-fitting jeans. With a sigh she slid it back—there hadn't been a signal since lunchtime and a couple of hours later the landline had gone too. It wasn't being cut off that was worrying Flora, it was her inability to contact her mother.

Under normal circumstances she wouldn't have been concerned about her parent; under *normal* circumstances her mother would be here helping to run the place and look after baby Jamie, while continuing to run her own pottery business. Multitasking was Grace Henderson's middle name and Flora wished she had a fraction of her resourceful parent's energy.

But these weren't normal circumstances. Her fiercely independent mother was operating on crutches with her leg in plaster and grieving deeply for her firstborn. Flora took comfort for the fact that, although the croft was remote, her mum had several good friends who lived close enough to be called neighbours who would no doubt have checked in on her.

Flora gnawed gently on her full lower lip as she weighed the option of putting more peat on the already smoking open fire before she went to bed. It was a matter of freeze or choke. She was trying to recall where the spare portable heaters she would need to put in the baby's room were stored, when there was a loud bang on the front door she had bolted after

Fergus had left, there being not much point the chef staying when all the diners had cancelled.

Feeling ashamed that her first thought was a selfish, *please don't wake the baby,* she rushed across the room, reading desperation into the loud urgent-sounding thuds. She fumbled with the door bolt, urgency making her fingers clumsy as the banging continued.

'Hold on, hold on, nearly...' As the door opened the wind blowing in off the sea loch that lapped the shore on the opposite side of the narrow road hit Flora with a full icy blast.

The physical force snatched the breath from her lips and made her stagger backwards, her arms flailing as she struggled to keep her balance. She barely heard the sound of the heavy oak door hitting the wall above the combined roar of the wind and the sound of invisible crashing waves feet away from the door.

It was to this wild soundtrack and out of the heavy swirling mist that the stranger entered.

He *was* a stranger... For one awful split second she'd thought *Callum*... It wasn't, of course. The local boy made good, thanks to an ability to kick a ball and increase the sales of everything from breakfast cereal to cars by smiling into the camera, lived in Spain—or was it Japan?—these days, and anyway there was no real resemblance beyond the impression of height, athletic muscularity, the dark hair and her imagination.

If it had been Callum she might have pushed him back out into the storm, but the man who *hadn't* broken her heart didn't look *pushable*!

He stood for a moment framed in the doorway, the top of his bare head touching the door frame, his broad shoulders filling the space as the long drover's-style overcoat he wore, caught by the wind, flared out behind him dramatically.

If this wild elemental storm had taken human form it would have looked like him.

Before her dazed brain could take in any more details he reached out, pulling the heavy door closed being him, making the effort of competing against the gale-force wind look effortless.

The deafening roar was instantly reduced to a dull distant moan and the fire, which had briefly flared to life with the influx of oxygen, died down as it blew out a cloud of acrid eye-stinging smoke, which under normal circumstances would have made Flora think about the damage it would inflict on the fresh white paintwork.

But she wasn't thinking about paintwork or actually anything else much. The adrenalin surge that held every muscle in her body taut to quivering point had thrown her nervous system directly into flight-or-fight mode, though neither would have done her much good against this man who, now the door was closed, seemed even taller.

He stood there for what felt like hours but might have been seconds, long enough at any rate for the details of his face to imprint themselves in her memory. The moisture that slicked his short dark hair against his skull trembled in droplets on the end of his dark, ludicrously long lashes and covered his face, making the olive-toned skin glow gold in the subdued lighting. Even if you had taken the incredible mouth and the dark deep-set eyes from the equation, the combination of hard planes and fascinating angles, emphasised by the shadow on his square jaw and hollow cheeks, was overtly sensual and overpoweringly male.

Refusing to acknowledge the hot sensation in her stomach as sexual awareness, she tried to kick free of the oddly hypnotic, cold, heavy-lidded eyes that held her own.

'Who are you?' she blurted when her vocal cords started working. Her voice lacked the welcoming Highland warmth that happy tourists frequently mentioned in their five-star reviews of the establishment, but, in her defence, she was in shock…or *something*?

She swallowed and brought her lashes down. Despite the protective sweep she continued to be conscious of those dark eyes with the glittering, deeply disturbing gold lights.

Oh, yes, she thought, grateful for the layers of clothing that muffled the sound of her heart hammering against her ribcage, this was *definitely* something. Not a big, significant something, just an 'opening of the door to find the most good-looking man she had ever seen or even dreamt existed standing there' something.

Was this a good time to discover that you still had a built-in weak spot for a pretty face? No, *Callum* had been *pretty*, this man was more…was *beautiful*. Too big a word…?

No, it wasn't, she decided, studying the perfect bone structure of his strongly carved face with its high carved cheekbones, square jawline and aquiline nose, her stomach dipping uncomfortably when she reached the sensual outline of his wide mouth.

Though actually what had really thrown her was the shock wave of overt sexuality his large presence in the low-ceilinged room created. The surface of her skin prickled with it and her knees were shaking.

Great! Just what she needed!

Fate decided losing her dearest sister and brother-in-law, inheriting their business and their baby son was not enough! Mr Dark and Brooding had to turn up on her doorstep and kick into life the embers of her dormant libido!

Admittedly, not dark and brooding's fault, but she struggled to view the intruder who, as supplying the *last* straw, she felt might just make her fold, with any objectivity.

Mouth closed might be a move in the right direction, Flora.

'I booked a room.'

His very low, deep voice had an almost tactile quality and held an intriguing almost accent. A wave of deep sadness tightened her throat—much deeper and harsher, but it reminded her a little of her late brother-in-law, Bruno. But Bruno's voice had been warm and filled with laughter; the stranger's voice held about the same amount of warmth as his cold dark eyes as he waited for her to respond.

She gave herself a mental shake, and dug deep into her reserves of professionalism. It wasn't normally an effort—she'd cut her hospitality teeth working shifts in a bar in Edinburgh when she was working her way through university. Several recent guests had commented online about her 'friendly efficiency and warmth'.

So why was she standing here like a tongue-tied idiot?

True, to date none of the guests she'd immediately felt at ease with had arrived wearing a suit that screamed designer beneath a long, equally expensive-looking coat that hung off shoulders a mile wide. And none had...no, she decided not to even *think* about the sexual aura he exuded, hoping that she'd wake up tomorrow after a good night's sleep and discover it was a sleep-deprivation thing. The odds of this happening were pretty good, because, though her ex-fiancé's opinion on most things counted for zero with her, on one thing he was probably right—she wasn't really a *sexual* person.

'Is there a problem?'

Beyond the inescapable fact, Ivo realised, that he

had made the mistake of nursing preconceptions, having them challenged made him feel slightly off balance—not something he was accustomed to.

He didn't intend to get accustomed to it.

He hadn't even realised until the door had opened that he'd been expecting a tall willowy blonde standing there. He'd not been imagining a petite redhead, a belt holding up her snug-fitting jeans around an impossibly narrow waist.

Ivo dug his hands deep into his pockets as his long brown fingers flexed in response to the mental image of them closing around the circumference. The slight but distinctly feminine sinuous curves above and below the belt sent a fresh slug of scorching heat through his body as he studied them again before he dragged his attention back to her face.

He couldn't pretend it was a hardship to look at the woman his grandfather had casually suggested he marry.

From nowhere an image of her floating down a church aisle in white came into his head but he pushed it away. The same way he pushed away any thought of marriage. It had seemed like an inevitable prospect, something he owed to the continuation of his name…but the existence of Bruno's child, the next generation, took the pressure off.

Ivo was here, yes, but not to marry anyone!

Was his alternative plan any less insane? Actually, 'plan' might be overstating it—more a play-it-by-ear than actual plan.

So, yes, *possibly* insane, but less insane than it had seemed around the same time he had seriously contemplated abandoning his car on a section of the road that was underwater about half a mile away.

Ivo didn't believe in fate, signs or divine intervention, but when you were driving along a road that was rapidly becoming a river a man, even one who prided himself on being rational, did start to wonder: was someone somewhere trying to tell him something?

And it wasn't the first snag!

Ivo prided himself on being adaptable but today had tested him. Since he'd set out this morning everything that could go wrong had. Engine problems shortly after they had taken off from the private airstrip had forced the pilot to turn back and make an emergency landing in Rome.

When he had finally landed in the replacement jet there had been no driver willing to make the journey up to Skye with weather warnings out advising only essential journeys being made.

Considering that his journey was essential, he had been privately pretty scornful of weather warnings in the British Isles, assuming they'd probably meant heavy drizzle.

His contempt had come back to bite him. He glanced down at his ruined handmade leather shoes—the elderly couple he'd rescued after they'd run off the road had treated him like a hero—not a good fit.

And now he was here and things were still not

going to plan. He focused the objectivity he was famed for—some called it coldness—on the heart-shaped face turned up to him.

To suggest that she was *not* beautiful—even taking into account that his taste in women had never run to petite and fragile—would not have been an objective assessment. He'd met women who were more beautiful, though none had possessed a heart-shaped face framed by wild Pre-Raphaelite curls, the deep titian interwoven with strands of lighter gold.

As unexpected as the vividly pretty heart-shaped face had been was the twist of hard desire he'd experienced when he'd first laid eyes on her.

Setting aside that visceral response, he continued to study the face that had drawn this reaction. It was a face that came complete with tip-tilted nose, a cute, curvy full mouth and wildly sexy and deep kitten-wide pansy-blue eyes framed by spiky, thick, straight lashes. There was the suggestion of a cleft in her pointed, determined small chin.

In response to his question, Flora lifted her eyes from the relative safety of mid-chest level. His hard stare was disconcerting.

'You're wearing a tie.'

She squeezed her eyes closed and thought, *Any moment now I'm going to say something that suggests I have more than two brain cells.*

Please make it soon!

When she opened them again he'd already unbelted his overcoat and a jacket button. The long brown fingers of his hand were smoothing the already smooth streak of his grey tie that stood out against the spotless background of white, a white made virtually transparent by its saturated condition.

She registered the shadow of dark body hair before she looked quickly away, ignoring the tingling tightness that extended even to the skin of her scalp.

'You have a dress code?'

Ignoring the sneery sarcasm in his question, though if they had had one it would have been waterproofs and walking boots, she reminded herself that it was her job to make their guests' stays happy ones, even the ones who were objectionable. Though to be fair she supposed that anyone who had negotiated the single-track-with-passing-places roads to get here, scary for the uninitiated in any weather, might have some excuse for feeling stressed.

Not that he looked stressed, quite the opposite. The aura he projected was of someone in charge, not someone who needed reassurance and sympathy. It was hard to imagine anyone offering him a cup of tea and very much easier, she mused as her eyes drifted to that mouth, to think of them offering him a more intimate form of comfort.

She tried to walk back from the image that flashed into her head—it didn't help the situation in any way imagining a man naked—and produced a half-decent professional smile. Though the effect was probably spoilt by baby sick on her shoulder...*again*.

'No, but we do have drying facilities if you venture out on the hills, though obviously not recommended in this weather,' she added hastily. It was amazing how sometimes you had to spell out the obvious and amazing how little respect some city types had for either the elements or the terrain of the island.

'Oh, and there are Ordnance Survey maps in all the bedrooms, though some of guests make use of a local mountain guide service. And if you're interested in geology there are some fascinating—'

'I'm not, and I have quite a good sense of direction.' It had enabled him to be one of only a handful of entrants to complete the arduous desert trek against the clock and the elements for charity, but perversely right now the only place it was taking him was the curve of her lush lips—every road led to the same place.

The awkward silence stretched. Flora filled it with a cheery, 'So, you're here for the fishing?' As much as they desperately needed the money, Flora found herself wishing that he wasn't here at all.

His jaw clenched. 'I'm not here for the fishing.'

Fighting the childish urge to tell him she wasn't really interested anyway, she smiled. 'Well, I hope you enjoy your stay.' She hesitated a moment before admitting, 'The truth is I wasn't aware we had any bookings. Have you come far?'

'Yes.'

I've had more interesting conversations with a brick wall, she thought, keeping her smile in place until she discovered he was staring at her hair. She fought and lost the impulse to lift a hand to smooth the tangled curls, which at some point today had come free of the tight, efficient ponytail. The time when she was working in Edinburgh and spent the twenty minutes required in the morning to religiously straighten it to a smooth, shiny, straight river seemed a million years ago.

Luxury in this life was applying some lip balm.

'Well, I think you're very brave to make the journey in this storm, or possibly very foolish…?' As the addition slipped past her guard she added a smile, which hopefully robbed the comment of insult.

You did have to wonder, though, who in their right mind made a journey in this weather, ignoring advice from every agency out there including the stretched police force, who were begging people not to make unnecessary journeys until the storm abated.

It took a special sort of arrogance, and on their brief acquaintance Flora suspected this man possessed that quality in abundance.

'Right, well, if you'd just like to check in? Card, or…' She looked towards the table where the old-fashioned leather ledger was kept beside a book inviting guests to add their hopefully complimentary comments.

The book and the flowers and twigs she'd arranged in the old zinc jug the previous day were there, but not the leather ledger.

Ivo watched as she pressed a finger to the groove

above her nose, her smooth brow puckering in concentration, but it was the dark purplish smudges
beneath her blue eyes that drew his attention. He
pushed away a waft of feeling that fell short of being
empathy but nevertheless was distracting.

And he didn't need any more distraction, he decided, the initial gut-punch reaction when the door
had opened to reveal a diminutive flame-haired figure still raising some uncomfortable red-line-crossed
feelings that he felt the need to rationalise. He had
clearly subconsciously been expecting a replica of
her sister, the tall willowy blonde who had bewitched
his brother, and he was still adjusting to the reality.
Add that to him not factoring in the possibility he
might find the woman that stood between him and
his nephew attractive.

He had acknowledged it now and moved on… It
would only be a problem if he allowed it to be.

And he wouldn't.

His confidence was justified: the last time Ivo had
allowed his libido to rule him he'd been a teenager
and his brother had not yet abandoned everything for
a woman. Ivo had been in lust a number of times but
had so far avoided anything that could be termed *in
love*. He'd never been in what people would call a
long-term relationship, because, in his experience,
before he'd ever got close to long term the woman
in his bed, who had begun by telling him how much
she *loved* him the way he was, had begun chipping

quietly away, trying to change what she had claimed to like about him.

A massive red line of a deal breaker; the woman did not exist that he would change for. The woman did not exist that he could not live without. Even the thought drew the corners of his lips into a cynical smile.

'You *are* the person in charge?'

His words brought Flora's chin up. Obviously this guy's personality was not as perfect as the rest of him.

'I am the person in charge,' she confirmed, sounding a lot calmer than she felt while she wondered what sort of write-up punching him on his nose would earn her.

Actually, during the past nightmare weeks, *in charge* was the last thing she had felt, but luckily she could put on a good act. She did so now as she walked confidently across to the bar, as if there were no doubt in her mind that she would find the old-fashioned bookings diary where it lay concealed on a shelf.

Luck was on her side.

'Here we are,' she said, laying it on the reclaimed wood surface.

The satellite dish meant to connect them to the Internet and the twenty-first century was arriving next week, which might make this old-fashioned ledger redundant. It was another of the outstanding bills that was keeping her awake nights.

She turned from the back where the restaurant bookings were written down, all this evening's cancellations highlighted by a red line drawn through them, to the front where room bookings were recorded. Sure enough, above one of the cancellations one of the rooms had been booked out for tonight.

She looked up, struggling to feel the professional warmth she had infused her smile with. 'I'm sorry I missed this one, Mr...?' She shook her head unable to decipher Fergus's scrawl or throw off the peculiarly strong antipathy the man had evoked in her.

'Rocco,' Ivo responded, giving his middle name as he had on the telephone when booking. He hadn't wanted to commit himself to a course of action before he'd read the situation.

'Right, Mr Rocco, sorry about the miscommunication and the welcome.'

'Or lack of it,' he inserted smoothly.

'Just so, afraid I'd assumed that everyone had cancelled due to the storm.'

His dark gold-flecked gaze slid to the window where relentless rain was lashing. 'You mean it's not always like this?'

The comment was delivered without the leavening humour which would have made it acceptable. Flora resisted the impulse to rush to the defence of her beloved home.

Her smile frayed a little at the edges as her sister's face floated into her head. Sami would have had this man eating out of her hand by now. She flinched at the physical impact as the fresh loss hit her all over again. She almost wished that Jamie would wake up so that she would have something practical to focus on to dull the pain. Maybe being too tired to think was not such a bad thing, she mused, ignoring the bleak voice in her head that told her she was only delaying the inevitable, she'd have to *feel* at some point.

'Would you like a wee dram to warm you after your journey?' She bent down to reach the forty-year-old single malt they kept behind the bar for occasions such as this.

The bottle of last resort, Bruno had called it, to be used when everything else failed with awkward or upset customers. They had very few of those, and so far it had been brought out to toast special occasions, like newly engaged couples.

Ivo watched, with what he told himself was academic interest, as the denim of the redhead's jeans stretched attractively over her taut, rounded rear as she bent over. There was nothing academic about the flash of heat down his front.

Flora straightened up, planted the bottle on the bar so that he could see the label, but his expression did not melt… *Could granite melt?* 'On the house, of course,' she added hastily.

'No.' The guest responded to the generous gesture with a look that flattened her smile. 'If I could see the menu?'

Her expression fell. 'Menu…?'

He arched a sardonic brow and watched the angry colour wash over the fair freckled skin.

She bit her lip. 'Fergus, the chef, has gone home actually…' She stopped. Was it such a good idea to tell this bad-tempered beautiful stranger with his indefinably menacing air that they were alone but for a baby lying asleep upstairs? Feeling ashamed of the sudden flurry of fear, she lifted her chin, squared her shoulders and added a very unconvincing, 'Sorry.'

'So your kitchen is closed?' *Of course it was.* Ivo had stopped trying to imagine the urbane sophisticated brother he remembered living in this cold, misty, uninviting backwater. He sent up a silent apology to his grandfather, who he had assumed was guilty of over-exaggeration when he'd described the place his great-grandson needed rescuing from. Ivo no longer needed convincing.

From his expression she could see there was no five-star rating heading their way. 'I could make you a sandwich?' It wasn't that she *couldn't* cook, but Flora was intimidated by the restaurant's industrial-looking catering kitchen with its shiny stainless-steel surfaces and latest top-of-the-range gadgets.

She didn't ask for a translation of the sound he made in his throat, quite happy to take it as a rejection.

'Right, then,' she said briskly. 'Shall I show you to your room? We're having a little storm-related problem with the heating,' she explained putting an awful lot of effort into the lie. It was glaringly obvious by his attitude that he didn't actually believe a word she was saying. 'But I'll bring up an electric heater and you'll be toasty in no time.' She crossed her fingers while making the over-optimistic prediction. 'If you'll follow me?'

One foot on the bottom step of the staircase, she stopped as the fire chose that moment to belch a fresh flume of acrid smoke that filled the entire room. Flora stopped cursing long enough to cough. 'The wind must be in the wrong direction,' she excused hoarsely.

'There is a right direction?' he asked sardonically.

Before she could react to the sarcasm she was distracted by a sighing sound broadcast from the baby monitor, followed by a sleepy murmur.

Ivo watched as the redhead literally held her breath for a full thirty seconds before her tense shoulders sagged with visible relief.

CHAPTER THREE

'YOU HAVE A CHILD?'

He watched the shock widen her eyes. Fascinated, Ivo observed the play of emotion across her fine-boned features. His fascination was mingled with disquiet that anyone could wear their emotions so close to the surface; the idea of exposing your vulnerabilities to the world the way she appeared to was anathema to Ivo.

When her reply came a moment or so later it was tinged with surprise underlain with a hint of defiance evident in the straightening of her slender shoulders.

'Yes, that is my child.'

Flora had accepted the doctor's verdict. It hadn't been easy, and for a time she had been angry, but she had come to terms with the fact her endometriosis was so bad that her fertility was severely impaired.

She could have carried on being angry and bitter or hoped for a medical miracle. She supposed it was one of those events in life that everyone reacted to differently. Her way had been to accept what had happened, and save her energy for fights she could win, not lost causes.

That didn't mean she hadn't dreamt of saying those words...*my child.*

Ironic that when she got to say them it wasn't because of a miracle or a dream-come-true scenario but because she was living a waking version of a nightmare Flora would have given everything she possessed *not* to be saying those words now, but when she did verbalising them brought home the full reality of the situation crashing in.

It was something that happened several times a day and each time the impact felt like walking into a wall of loss and pain, and, yes, fear that she just wasn't up to the job.

Flora had never felt more desperately inadequate to any task in her life. Sure, her career had held challenges, and some were scary with an inbuilt possibility of failure, but this was different. *Parenthood* was different. Being responsible for a life was the scariest thing she had ever imagined. Could any training prepare you for it?

Or were good mothers born?

Sami had been one of those, she thought, her eyes misting as she thought of her sister, who had made it look so easy. Pushing her way through the jumble of conflicting emotions, she took a deep breath.

Doubts were distractions she couldn't afford. She needed to stay in 'one foot in front of the other' mode, and firmly focused on mundane things like paying the bills and staying awake!

Feelings and doubts were a luxury she didn't have time for.

'Oh, sorry,' she said brightly. 'Can I take your bag?' She glanced towards the overnight holdall he had dropped inside the door when he'd arrived.

Even standing on the second step, she had to tilt her head back to look him in the face. The action made her bright hair spill backwards in a tangled silky coil down her narrow back.

He knew from the file Salvatore had compiled—his grandfather was nothing if not thorough—that Flora Henderson had been forced by the recent tragic events to walk away from what was probably her dream job. He'd anticipated there might be resentment he might utilise to achieve his objective, that the role thrust on her might make her vulnerable.

Yes, she was, it was there to see in the hollows in her smooth cheeks, the shadowed unhappiness reflected in the shocking blue of her eyes and the dark circles underneath.

Yet instead of feeling satisfaction Ivo was conscious of something that came close enough to compassion to jolt him free of those blue eyes. A moment later he reassessed his reaction. Compassion required a degree of caring, and he did not care for this woman; there was nothing *personal* between them.

He only did personal with family and, aside from his grandfather, his only family now was the child sleeping upstairs. This woman stood between him and that child.

'I think I'll manage, Ms…?'

'Oh, it's Henderson.' Then, because they were listed on all the websites as providing a relaxed, informal environment, she fought her innate reluctance to provide this man with any personal details and added, 'Flora.' Facing ahead, she started up the stairs, not needing the creak behind her to tell he was following. The hairs on the back of her neck told her that.

By the time they reached the top she was breathless, in part because she had attacked them like an athlete out to break records, but mostly because of the unnerving way he had looked at her, as though he could see inside her head.

They reached the top and she paused, opening the door of the store cupboard at the top and reaching in to pull out an electric fan heater, relieved to be able to look efficient, or at least slightly less inefficient. No need for him to know that she had only remembered where they were stored halfway up the stairs.

'Your room is the other side of the house.' Flora tucked the light heater under her arm and pushed aside a tendril of red hair that was tickling her nose. 'So, hopefully you won't be disturbed. Fingers crossed.'

'That's a very scientific attitude to customer service.'

Flora smiled through gritted teeth, rather glad she

had only imagined the sympathy she had seen in his face. 'We aim more for the warm personal touch.' *Not* that *personal, Flora,* said the voice in her head when she realised the she was staring at the firm, sensual outline of his mouth. 'If you'd like to follow me, Mr Rocco,' she offered primly.

The selection of the room farthest from the nursery had seemed a good choice. It was the biggest and it had the best views; the size meant tonight it was also the coldest.

'I hope you'll be comfortable,' she huffed, watching her warm breath mist in the cold air as she bent forward to plug in the heater before switching it to the maximum setting. 'It'll warm up in no time,' she promised him optimistically.

'So, tea and coffee making facilities.' Her fluttering gesture indicated the tray complete with cafetière on a side table. She picked up the tin beside it. 'The shortbread is homemade.' Most guests looked impressed by this; he didn't, but Flora doggedly persevered despite the lack of reaction. *Heavens, would it kill him to smile?* 'Drinks and milk in the fridge,' she added, ticking off the items in her head. She opened the wardrobe door. 'Fresh robe and extra towels and blankets. Just let us know when you check out what you had. The prices are the same as the bar. I hope you have a comfortable night, Mr Rocco,' she said formally as she backed towards the door. 'Oh, would you like a hot-water bottle tucked in your bed?'

If there was anything he would like tucked...

He stopped the thought dead but had no control over the blood-warming image that followed in its wake, an image that involved him being warmed by her smooth limbs wrapped around him. A slow steady throb of heat slid through his body. When he was finally able to force the words out past the lustful fog that had seeped into his head, his voice had a throaty rasp.

'Do I look like I need a hot-water bottle, Flora?' What he needed was some resistance to the magnetic pull of her plump rose-coloured lips.

His grandfather's plan might have involved seduction but his wouldn't. Emotions complicated things, and expecting someone who showed every nuance of emotion on her face to have any degree of emotional continence was unrealistic.

His plan would be a business deal plain and simple...in theory at least. He was beginning to wonder if this woman could do plain and simple. Was she capable of looking through anything without distorting the image through an emotional prism?

It was his task to make sure she did. He didn't doubt his ability to make this happen and, given the fact her options were limited, it should not be difficult.

His delivery was deadpan, the tone sardonic, but it was the predatory glow in his dark eyes... She wanted to look away. She wanted to run from the room in which the *uncomfortable* factor in the atmosphere she'd coped with up to this point by simply pretending it didn't exist had hiked up several notches.

Ignoring was no longer an option.

But growing a backbone was.

Focusing on the sound of distant alarm bells and not the ache in her stomach, she lifted her chin and wrenched her eyes free of his molten stare. Or was it molten? Was she just seeing what she wanted to?

The mortifying idea that she *wanted* him to look at her that way cooled the sexual pulse that beat low and hot in her belly. Her initial antipathy had not been irrational but spot on. Her chin lifted. He might remind her of a sleek, well-fed predator, but she was damned if she was going to act like some little cowering mouse for his amusement.

Hope you freeze!

For one awful moment she thought she'd voiced the vicious and uncharitably spiteful thought out loud. She *almost* felt ashamed. She was neither vicious nor spiteful.

'Goodnight, Mr Rocco.'

Flora waited until she had cleared the guest wing of the house before she leaned against the wall and released the tension that had her body in a stranglehold grip in a series of long hissing sighs.

Her legs felt like lead as she went back to the store cupboard and pulled out the heaters for Jamie's room; her energy levels seemed to have seeped away along with the tension. She headed for the baby's room. There were no heaters left for her own bedroom but then cooling down was probably not such a bad idea.

On tiptoe, barely breathing, Flora plugged the heaters in one of the sockets in Jamie's room. She looked at the sleeping baby, the swell of love that tightened in her chest physically painful.

She might be a poor substitute for what he had lost but she was *determined* to give this baby all the love his parents would have if they had lived. If only, she mused wistfully, there were a handbook somewhere for people who had zero parenting skills.

Her mum was there to help and pass on her parenting skills and Flora was thankful for that, but she was also reluctant to rely on her too much. It was easy to forget sometimes, given her very youthful outlook and zest for life, that Grace Henderson had had her share of health problems. Typically, she played them down but losing Sami had taken a massive emotional toll and then she'd had her own accident… No, her mum needed to be resting and healing, not running to the aid of her pathetic daughter, which was why Flora had been glossing over any difficulties she was having and not confiding her doubts. She would tell her mum about the nightmare financial problems she had inherited after she had worked out a solution… *or they foreclosed on the mortgage.*

Pushing away the depressing thought, she took one last look at the sleeping baby, wondering if it was possible the baby just *knew* there was an amateur in charge, that at some instinctive baby level he knew that the two people who loved him most were gone.

But he'd know his parents; they would be real people to him. Flora had already begun putting items, photos and mementos in a memory book to show him when he was older. She had pasted photos of her sister growing up on the first few pages; she just wished she had more memories of his father to put in.

'Sleep tight,' she whispered, checking the red light on the baby monitor one last time before she quietly left the room, then slipping downstairs for a last-minute check. She switched off the outside light and peered through the window just as the moon appeared through the clouds.

Her stomach gave a little lurch of dismay and her eyes grew round in horror as the silver light revealed the water level; the waves were lapping in the middle of the road just feet from the low wall.

Was this the perfect storm moment, the once every twenty years that they would flood?

She pushed away the thought. She was not the sort of person who assumed the worst, though, after the worst had happened to their family, her built-in optimism was feeling more than a little battered and bruised. It was weariness and not optimism that enabled her to dismiss the potential disaster and make her way up the stairs.

With the heater turned up full the room became, if not *toasty* as his hostess had optimistically predicted, at least tolerably warm enough to make him feel able to strip down to his shorts before he got into the surprisingly comfortable bed with the pristine white sheets.

His head had barely made an indent in the pillow before he heard the sound, the soft but unmistakable sound of a baby's cry above the sounds of the storm that continued to rage outside.

Ten minutes later the baby was still crying.

Did healthy babies cry this much?

Ivo had always possessed the ability to tune out background noise and distractions. He could sleep anywhere—at least he'd thought so. But it turned out there was a nerve-shredding noise that he couldn't tune out. Twice over the next half an hour the sound stopped only to start up again just as he had been lulled into a false sense of security and relaxed.

When it happened a third time he snapped; throwing back the quilt, he bounced out of bed and over to the door.

The temperature in the hallway was several degrees colder than his room. At some point, he supposed, this had seemed like a good idea, if for no other reason than anything was better than lying there listening to the racket that was driving him crazy. *Now you'll just look crazy!*

Quite suddenly the noise stopped. Aware it could be another false alarm, he didn't relax, neither did he turn around and crawl into his comfortable bed and get what sleep he could. He was committed to the course of action that took his feet towards the flickering light he could see spilling out into the hallways ahead.

The compulsion that drove him was stronger than logic. His brother's child, his nephew, was inside that room, the only part of Bruno that remained.

When he reached it, the door was ajar. On well-oiled hinges it swung silently inwards when he touched it. The room it revealed was small, painted a bright in-your-face yellow. The heat blasting out from the heaters that were positioned either end of it made the mobiles hanging from the ceiling spin, bringing the clowns and seals and cats to life. The effect when you added the stars and moons the night light projected on the ceiling was all a little surreal.

Ivo barely noticed.

His attention was completely focused on the spot where Flora Henderson was standing, her back turned to him, for the moment oblivious of his presence. She was holding the child, who seemed to be sleeping now; all he could see was the dark curly top of his head and his legs encased in blue, hanging limp.

He watched as she walked barefoot across the room to where the cot was situated under a curtained window. She was wearing a thin blue cotton nightdress that ended just below her knees and was held up by thin straps that revealed the curve of her delicate shoulder blades. The fabric billowed a little as she walked, allowing him to see the narrowness of her waist and the firm curves of her bottom through it.

Later, when he examined the moment he viewed it in the light of a long, very bad, incredibly frustrating day, but at that moment he could not apply logic to the scalding heat of the hormone rush that blanked his mind totally. Just wiped it clean of everything but the sense-destroying lust that for a few moments utterly consumed him.

He had begun to claw his way back to a semblance of control when she lifted her head, the upper half of her body half turning towards him, allowing him a view, through the gaping neck of her nightdress, of the smooth slopes of her breasts and the darker shadow of her nipples through the fabric. Their glances connected, blue on black, and he felt the control he had fought for slipping through his fingers like a wet rope burning flesh as he clung on.

Then he saw the wetness on her face, absorbed the evidence of tears that she didn't seem conscious of and the gleam of intent in his eyes faded. He swallowed.

'Let me help.' Ivo had no idea where the words came from; he was immune to female tears.

So why was he reacting to them now?

The answer threw up a lot more difficult questions.

He'd first set eyes on the woman a couple of hours ago so how could he be so sure, so absolutely bet-your-life-on-it positive, that the tears were not there to gain sympathy? Why did he *know* she'd crawl before she'd ask for help?

Flora's chin went up in response. She opened her mouth, the huffy rejection ready to deliver with the right degree of 'I can take care of myself' ice, when on her shoulder the baby shifted and gave a sleepy sigh.

She reacted automatically, shifting his weight so that he lay against her chest in the crook of her right arm. She flexed the fingers of her left hand, still numb and tingling from the time she had taken his weight there.

Oh, God, what was she doing, and what place did pride have in the situation? She needed a helping hand even if that hand, with the long tapering brown fingers, did seem to exert a weird and worrying fascination. Help, even if it came from a totally unexpected and frankly disturbing quarter, was still help.

And on the plus side, accepting his offer would mean hopefully he'd vanish a lot quicker.

And Flora needed him to vanish. He was too big and too…*everything* for the room. His presence seemed to alter the constituents of the air she was breathing, making it heavy, making breathing require a conscious effort.

'I have kind of lost the feeling in my left arm. If you could just pull the cot sheet back?' Her chin resting on Jamie's dark curls, she stretched out, letting out a tiny but revealing gasp as her hand felt the brush of his long brown fingers.

The electrical surge that made her eyes widen left her knees feeling weak and reawakened the shivery sensation that had originally alerted her to his presence a few heavy heartbeats before she actually saw him standing there, carrying off the tumbled-out-of-bed look like only your average sex god could.

She supposed that she should be grateful that he didn't sleep naked, though the boxer shorts he wore were not substantial enough to help her!

'Thank you.'

She had no defence mechanism to deal with the compulsion to stare at his long, lean, golden, totally magnificent body. There was not an ounce of surplus flesh to hide the perfect definition of his toned body. Her eyelids fluttered and her throat grew dry as her glance slid again over the broadness of his muscled shoulders and chest to the slabbed muscles of his belly. His legs were long, the muscular thighs slightly dusted with dark hair. The same dark hair that formed a directional arrow that vanished beneath the waistband of his boxer shorts.

Pulling in a sharp, tense breath, Flora lifted her gaze and found it connecting with his, dark shadowed and deeply disturbing. His olive skin looked warm, his carved mouth looked... She blinked hard and took a step back like someone who had just discovered they were standing on the edge of a precipice, which explained the dizziness.

He watched her lift a fluttering hand to her face, looking bemused as it came away wet. She frowned at her fingers, not seeming to make the connection between the salty moisture and her own tears.

He didn't know if the tiny negative shake of her head was aimed at herself or him, and a moment later her expression was hidden from view, the silky curtain of her flame-red hair falling in an abundant cloud as she bent forward to lay the sleeping baby into the cot, fumbling with the crumpled sheet as she tried to pull it back.

'Let me.'

Without waiting for a response, he pulled back the tangled sheet she had been struggling with, smoothing it back so that she could lay the baby down on his back.

As the baby lay there clenching and unclenching this pudgy fists, Ivo had his first proper look at his nephew, hungry to see a resemblance to his brother in the unformed features. He felt a strange tightness in his chest as he took in the details: dark hair, a snub nose and pale pink skin, eyes tightly closed, untouched by life yet and *totally* perfect.

So vulnerable.

Your father would have died for you, he thought.

Better Bruno had lived.

'I…thank you.' The light brush of his fingers lasted longer than it should this time. As for the stomach-clenching shudder that felt as though it would never go away even after his hand had moved and he had straightened up…

She took longer than she needed to smooth the

sheet over the baby, giving herself some time to recover from the primal reaction that had convulsed her body when she'd seen him standing there, a confusing combination of heart-thudding excitement and fear blurred into one.

'You must be cold,' she blurted stupidly.

His mobile lips twitched into a wicked smile that made her stomach lurch.

The man looked like a fallen angel on steroids!

The impression intensified as he spread his arms wide, then slowly he glanced down, an expression of comical injured dismay on his ludicrously handsome chest. 'You have very high standards, *cara*.'

The softly drawled *cara* hit her reasoning functions dead centre, delaying her deciphering of the softly seductive insinuation.

When his meaning hit she wanted to crawl under a stone. Instead she lifted her chin and, hampered by the need to keep the noise down, whispered, 'I didn't mean…' She stopped. Of course he knew what she didn't mean. *'Funny!'* She sniffed, slinging him an unamused glance as she moved away from the cot containing the sleeping baby.

He followed her; the combination of handsome, half-naked, totally gorgeous man and small room was enough to make anyone hyperventilate. She resisted the impulse to pick a cushion from the rocker and wield it defensively. Instead she pressed a hand to her chest and willed her breathing to slow. 'I'm sorry if I disturbed you.'

It was the next best thing to pushing him through the door, an obvious signal for him to go; it was equally obvious he didn't recognise it as such. She ground her teeth in frustration and, seriously, he had to be cold by now. Despite the unbidden thought, by some miracle she kept her eyes above waist level, though the effort raised her own internal temperature by several uncomfortably shameful degrees.

She took another step towards the door and reached across to switch the lamp off, before turning the dimmer on the night light down. The room was now lit by the soft soothing silhouettes of moons and stars revolving on the ceiling.

'So, goodnight, Mr Rocco,' she said softly.

He saw the dismissal in her smile and, while part of him recognised walking away was a good idea, he just couldn't let it go and he didn't have a clue why!

She hadn't quite reached the door when his soft voice brought her to a halt.

'You've been crying.'

Her eyes flew to his face, her first instinct to deny this crazy assertion. It was a reflex. People looked at her and saw fragile; she wasn't, and if it meant acting a bit tougher than she actually was to show them how wrong they were it was a price worth paying.

Fast on the first instinct and overpowering it in a heartbeat was the realisation that letting her guard down to someone who didn't know her, and who couldn't care less, someone who wasn't going to lose sleep over anything, might be the outlet she needed.

In any event the internal debate was useless because the words came of their own volition.

'It was the blinds.' Her eyes went to the blinds with their cheery fabric of sailboats and balloons, drawn to cut out the darkness beyond. Flora had her own darkness inside and there was no hiding from that. She felt as though she'd never feel light again.

Only crazy people wept buckets about window dressings. She wouldn't have blamed him if he'd made a dash for the door—it would save her making any more of a fool of herself than she had already.

But he didn't.

'Sami, my big sister, she made them—she could make anything!' Her smile dissolved into a gulp as she rushed on. 'We shopped for the material...' It had been a girls' day out in Edinburgh. 'We had lunch, too many cocktails—it was a perfect day.'

Her big blue eyes lifted to his. It was all there for him to see: the pain, the grief, the aching sense of loss. He didn't *want* to see it but he couldn't stop looking and listening to her beautifully accented, hushed voice.

'Only I didn't know that at the time or I would have...' Her voice trailed away.

'Cherished it?'

Her eyes flew wide in acknowledgement.

'It seems to me you did.' He could have had moments to cherish but... Jaw clenched, he pushed away the thought, unwilling to allow himself the indulgence of self-pity.

He couldn't change history; he couldn't have that day with his brother; he couldn't be part, even for a short time, of the small family that had been so cruelly ripped apart, but he could be there for Bruno's son.

What do you *know about families?* sneered the voice in his head.

He turned a deaf ear to the voice and focused on the memory of that almost visceral rush of protectiveness he had felt when he'd seen the baby. Nothing else really mattered.

'I miss her and Jamie is missing her, too. I know he is.' Her glance swivelled to the sleeping baby, perceptibly softening as she did so. 'He's her son, not mine.' Her glance lifted from the baby to briefly touch his lean dark face.

He's a stranger—why are you telling him this?

Because he is a stranger.

'Hers and Bruno's.' Still looking in the direction of the cot, she didn't see his reaction to her mention of her brother-in-law's name, the flicker of pain that crossed his handsome face. 'I'm trying, but I don't really think I'm cut out for this. Any of it.' She had dodged the truth for so long that to say it out loud, to acknowledge it, was a massive relief. 'I make a *terrible* mother.'

The confession should, under the circumstances, have been music to his ears. Instead as Ivo looked into those tear-filled, tragic, beautiful eyes he was conscious of a totally alien and dangerous instinct to offer comfort.

He didn't like the feeling; the effort of combatting it made the muscles round his strong jaw quiver.

Flora's chest felt tight as she struggled to hold in the sob she could feel building inside her.

She was winning the battle when he touched her face. The shock of the contact melted through her, each subsequent ripple of sensation making her insides dissolve warmly. She wanted to look away but his thumb was lodged in the angle of her jaw, framing her face, his finger on her cheek.

'It must be tough…alone…' He silenced the sudden stab of guilt with the reminder that everything he had seen told him that his decision to take Bruno back to Italy was the right one. This woman was drowning under the weight of responsibility, and she'd thank him in the long run. Not that he wanted her thanks, he just wanted Bruno's son back where he belonged.

'You *are* alone…?'

Flora nodded, touched despite herself by his understanding. She had actually never felt more alone in her life.

She blinked. His chest was just there, warm and hard and solid. In her head she saw herself laying her face against his skin, feeling his arms wrap around her, resting just for a moment.

She turned her cheek into his big hand. It was a good fit; his fingers were cool against her skin. It felt like a dream and any moment now she'd wake up.

Did she want to?

Had he stepped in closer? Had she? Flora realised she had no idea but she was breathing hard and feeling light-headed as she stared up into his eyes, the swell of feeling to let go inside her surging upwards... She stepped forward, this time consciously.

The floorboard beneath her feet creaked and she froze, the sound breaking her free of the sexual thrall that had held her a willing victim...and that was the shame of it: she'd been willing. So needy she would have accepted comfort from a total stranger.

Burning with shame, she turned, and with a mumbled, *'Sorry,'* dashed for the door, picking up a throw from the chair as she went.

After a moment Ivo followed her, closed the door behind him and watched as she wrapped the blanket and her dignity around herself like a protective shield.

'I have to tell you that I don't normally—' She stopped and thought.

I don't have to tell because he almost certainly doesn't want to know, and, let's face it, the man could probably fill a book with things he really doesn't want to know about you at this point, Flora.

'Sleep deprivation. Long day. Teething...'

Could you sound more certifiably insane if you tried, Flora? she asked herself in despair.

The last word drew his attention to her teeth, the neat white upper set, which were at that moment gouging a groove in the soft-flesh plumpness of her lower lip.

'Sexual frustration…?' It was with something of a relief that Ivo diagnosed his own aberrant behaviour.

She reacted to the slow sibilant suggestion by jerking to attention. 'Pardon?' He either didn't hear the ice in her tone, or didn't care.

'Well, it's got to be tough living all the way out here? Men are pretty scarce, I am assuming? Not what you're used to. You must miss your old life, the buzz of living in a city, friends, galleries, theatre and…'

She pulled herself up to her full height of five three and glared huffily across at him, too consumed by the battle with her own embarrassment to notice the colour scoring the angle of his high cheekbones. 'Are you suggesting I was…was…*hitting* on you? And how do you know I lived in the city?'

One sable brow lifted as he looked into her cobalt-blue eyes. Nothing in his face suggested he was anything other than mildly amused by what had happened.

'My mistake,' he drawled.

She screwed up her eyes and glared. 'I'd have to be a lot more desperate than I am to—' She stopped, a look of dismay that in other circumstances Ivo might have found amusing spreading across her face. 'Not that I am desperate, that is…' She saw his lips twitch and thought, *He's laughing at me.*

And you're surprised?

She opened her mouth and closed it again, remembering the advice her mother had been giving her since she was a little girl with a red-headed temper.

Flora, when you're in a hole that's over your head, stop digging!

It was a lesson she still hadn't learnt.

'We are not exactly a cultural desert here, you know, and…goodnight, Mr Rocco.'

'Goodnight, *Ms* Henderson.' The heavy, hot desire pooled in his groin suggested this would not be a good night for him.

CHAPTER FOUR

IVO HAD EVENTUALLY fallen asleep at about four a.m., and when he woke it took him a few moments to realise what was different and then it came to him—it was the absence of noise.

It was totally silent.

The light shining through the edges of the closed blackout blind revealed a room he hadn't been in any mood to appreciate last night. The colour scheme was pale and soothing, shades of white and grey with splashes of colour in the art on the walls, which looked to be original. Besides the very comfortable and adequate-sized oak platform bed, the furniture was an eclectic mix of old and new. The exposed oak boards looked original and were softened by hand-woven rugs. A massive hand-thrown pot set on a slate washstand was filled with artistically arranged driftwood.

It was all a million miles away from the sleek modernity and uniformity of the professionally staged luxury hotel rooms he usually used as he travelled the world.

But unlike last night, this morning he was able to see the appeal. It was not hard to see why this place was popular, an opinion based not just on the ambience but the financial accounts his grandfather had *acquired*. It had a lot going for it, but Bruno had made the classic mistake of overextending himself. He'd left very little wriggle room, which meant the moment the unexpected had happened there had been a domino effect.

The unexpected had been a rise in the interest rates and—well—the fatal accident.

The place had closed for several weeks after the accident, which had punched a massive hole in the fragile cash-flow, and the situation had rapidly gone from bad to worse. Customers put off by the idea of new management had started cancelling their bookings.

The reputation could, of course, be rebuilt but not without a healthy cash flow. Without a massive injection of capital the place would go under; it was inevitable. Ivo was not sentimental about such things but he suspected, actually he was relying on the fact, that Flora Henderson was.

It seemed a safe bet.

An image of her expressive face drifted into his head.

More, it was a sure thing, he decided, a hint of disapproval turning down the corners of his mouth as he stretched to relieve the kinks in his spine and curved one hand above his head. It was a comfortable position to go over the events of last night, supported by a very comfortable mattress and safe this morning behind the wall of emotional isolation that had taken him years to build.

And one moment, one tear, one sniff, one trembling lip, to knock down.

He pushed the thought away.

It had been a perfect storm moment, and he wasn't going to make the mistake of reading too much into it. He left that to people who thought there was more to attraction than chemistry. He was not one of those people, and this morning his mind was functioning with its usual clarity and his objectivity was in place.

Lucky, because if the plan is to work you'll need to keep an emotional distance from the redhead!

It took Flora ten indulgent minutes to blur the worst of the ravages left by a sleepless night...only thirty seconds to scrub it all away; after all, she had nothing to prove to anyone, least of all a guest.

She was on her second cup of coffee when the kitchen back door opened. The farmer from the neighbouring farm stood there, a ladder casually balanced on his shoulder.

'Rough night.'

She started guiltily, the horror in her eyes giving way to embarrassment as she realised what he meant. 'Oh, the weather, you mean.'

'You've got a few slates loose, lass.'

The comment drew a laugh from Flora. 'You're not the first to suggest it.'

He grinned and half turned. 'Won't take long. See you've got a guest.' He nodded towards the small car park where a top-of-the-range car splattered with mud and complete with some spectacular scratches to the paintwork was parked beside her own battered four-wheel drive, which had so many dings that a few more weren't to be noticed.

Flora nodded.

'Ah, well, it all helps.'

Flora nodded again and wondered if *everyone* on the island knew about her financial problems. The answer, she knew, was probably. There were advantages and disadvantages to living in such a small community; secrets were a very rare commodity.

But when you needed help you didn't have to ask, she mused, deciding to delay ringing her mum until later—she might be having a lie-in.

She walked out into the bar area carrying cutlery to lay up a breakfast table, mentally practising the smooth, professional, just a little bit distant attitude she would take with her guest this morning.

She had no idea what she'd been thinking about, spilling everything like that. The memories made her cringe. The only solution to her embarrassment she had come up with was to pretend selective amnesia.

Well, what choice did she have? The option of taking the moral high ground was obviously off the table because if he had crossed any line she had virtually invited him to!

She squeezed her eyes closed in an effort to shut

out the mortifying memories of her emotional out-
pouring and the strange intimacy of those moments.

Like the forced intimacy of two people with nothing in common, who were shipwrecked and…hell,
there was no *forced* about it! Grimacing, she opened
her eyes just in time to stop herself colliding with
the tall figure from last night.

Standing with his back to her, he didn't immediately react to her exclamation; when he did turn
around she saw what he was holding.

'That's my sister and her husband. Jamie was just
hours old.' She held out her hand for the framed
photo, resisting the impulse to snatch it from him.

'They look happy.' Ivo put the framed photo of
the smiling couple holding a newborn in her hand
and watched as she stroked the frame before replac-
ing it on the shelf where he had seen it when he'd
walked into the room.

Flora swallowed, feeling the anger rise up inside
her like a wave. It was unfair—just so unfair. Why
them? Her chest heaved with the silent effort of pushing those feelings back down. Newsflash: life wasn't
fair—it sucked, end of story. She didn't have time to
be bitter and twisted; she had a baby to care for and
a business to save.

She felt those dark eyes on her and unconsciously
straightened her shoulders before turning around.
'They were,' she said softly. 'I think they were the
happiest people I know.' She made a throat-clearing
sound before adding formally, 'So sorry we disturbed

you last night, Mr Rocco.' *But not as much as you disturbed me,* she thought as an image floated into her head of him standing there in the doorway like a bronzed statue. Tthe memory was enough to create a rippling sensation low in her pelvis.

'It's Ivo.'

She acknowledged this with a slightly wary tip of her head, her brow furrowing as she wondered why that name seemed familiar. The answer was right there, then he spoke, and it vanished.

Ivo's dark brows drew into a critical dark line above his aquiline nose as he took in her pallor, and the dark shadows. 'Did you get *any* sleep?' The flash of concern in his head was filtered into accusation by the time it left his lips.

Her lips tightened under his critical scrutiny. So she looked like a wreck—did he imagine she needed telling? He, of course, looked as though he'd had a full eight hours; you could almost feel the vitality he oozed from every perfect pore. He was probably one of those irritating people who only needed an hour's sleep, she decided, nursing her resentment.

'Yes, thank you,' she lied, experiencing a flash of shame as she recalled the very little sleep she had had. Luckily for her peace of mind, only snatches of the dreams remained. *A girl can't take responsibility for her unconscious mind,* she reminded herself.

The excuse didn't really stand up to scrutiny when a moment later she found herself studying him through the sweep of her lashes. Her *conscious* mind was definitely in control as she took in the length of his legs in a pair of dark jeans and the lean, whip-cord strength of his upper body showcased in a close-fitting steel-grey cashmere sweater. He looked good with clothes on too.

Head bent to hide the shamed flush that burned her smooth cheeks pink, she fiddled with the break-fast menu she had inserted into the basket of cutlery, before formally motioning him to a table beside the window that had the best view of the loch, blue, calm and beautiful on the morning that was clear enough to see the distant mainland shore.

She cleared her throat. This was always going to be awkward but she could cope. 'Or you could eat in the dining room if you prefer.' She gave a too bright smile and nodded towards an open door to her left.

It was a strange feeling to look around and think of his high-powered executive brother living here. Had he been content, happy? Had he regretted his decision to give up everything for love?

Ivo felt the flash of something that he refused to acknowledge, even to himself, was anything even vaguely related to envy as he looked around the place that had been his brother's home.

'Where would you prefer?'

At the sound of Flora's voice the ghost images of his imagination faded.

From what he could see of the room she indicated it was less dining room and more alcove, but like the rest of the place it was tastefully and eclectically furnished, the walls lined with original local artwork that had adorned all the walls he'd seen. The note beneath the ones in his bedroom had bios of the artists, and sale prices.

'Here will be fine.'

'There might be a bit of noise.'

He glanced at the road. So far this morning he'd seen more sheep wandering along it than cars—at last count two and a tractor.

'The sheep?'

Her lips tightened at the sarcasm. 'Gregory is on the roof.'

His brows lifted. 'Did he forget to take his meds or is this a quaint local custom?'

Distracted by the drift of clean male scent that tickled her nostrils, she failed to react to his attempt at humour.

'Storm damage.'

Not the only sort of damage, he thought as he studied the extent of the violet shadows of exhaustion under her beautiful eyes. The sunlight exaggerated the pallor of her skin; by contrast it made her burnished hair shine like a beacon. The combination of fragility and heat shook some nameless feeling loose in his chest.

Nameless or not, it made him uneasy…in a different way from the unease, not to mention frustration, the blind primal lust he'd experienced last night had made him feel.

'We lost a few slates last night, it seems,' she explained.

She felt a tiny spurt of relief when her brief explanation drew his glance towards the window. In her book anywhere that wasn't her face was good or at least an improvement; good would be when this disturbing guest had got into his top-of-the-range car and driven away.

It was really weird that when he looked at her with those dark eyes she felt naked… Or was that she *thought* about getting naked? asked the sardonic voice in her head.

Ivo took a step closer to the window. It overlooked the same view as the one he'd lifted the blinds to in his bedroom earlier, but from a slightly different angle.

This morning it was easier to see why this island was such a popular tourist destination. There was no doubt the scenery was stunning in an untamed way.

Hard to believe that this was even the same planet, let alone the same godforsaken spot on the map he had driven to the previous night through what had seemed like a barren moonscape of mist and rock.

The crashing waves had gone; the whirls of light mist that, with the curlew cries, had given the scene an eerie quality earlier had gone. Now the tranquil waters of the loch were totally still. The surface so mirror calm that the sentinel purple-tinged mountains to the west were reflected on the surface.

There was little to show that there ever had been a storm except for one of the branches and collective detritus along the middle of the narrow single-track road—presumably the meandering line marked the level the waters had eventually reached last night.

'Do you ever flood here?'

He was looking at her again but Flora was ready and she gave a smile that was almost cool and collected. She was in charge of very little in her life at the moment but she was damned if she'd allow her renegade hormones to get the better of her.

'Every ten years or so.'

His elevated brows suggested scepticism but Flora felt on safe ground. Bruno and Sami had needed a report on flooding risks before they'd got planning permission. They had also needed an archaeological survey, which had suggested that people had lived in this spot for centuries.

'So is there much storm damage to the building?'

'I haven't looked yet but the place is pretty solid.'

'You just took a passing tradesman's word that you're missing slates. Did you even get a quote for their work?' His frown deepened as he considered her appalling naivety. Of course, that same flaw was going to make his task easier. *Or maybe not,* he thought as he watched her chin go up at a pugnacious angle.

'He's not a passing anything, he's a neighbour and a friend. Not all people put a price on everything,' she informed him scornfully. Gregory would be offended if she offered to pay him but he would take one of the jars of honey from their bees.

'Boyfriend?' he speculated.

The suggestion drew a gurgle of laughter from her throat. 'Gregory is married,' she retorted, more amused than huffy this time, and when she grinned the little cleft in her chin deepened in a way he found he quite liked. He couldn't remember the last time that he'd seen a woman with no make-up at all. He admired her soft creamy skin. He decided that the sheer novelty value alone would account for his fascination with the sprinkling of freckles across the bridge of her nose.

How far do those freckles go? he wondered as his eyes slid as though drawn by a magnet to the neckline of her top, to the striped sweater that clung to her soft curves.

'Can I get you tea or coffee?'

His eye lifted, the thin stripes of colour banding his cheekbones hardly visible as his nostrils flared as he breathed in the aroma coming from the kitchen.

'Coffee.' He watched as she bustled away, enjoying her rear view but in a much less pure way than he had enjoyed the view from the window.

When the coffee came he was prepared for the worst but it was better than awful, which was a plus.

'I need to talk to you.'

Flora froze in 'deer in the headlights' mode, only just biting back the *Oh, God, no!* 'Last night was not...me...nothing...'

'I do not wish to discuss what happened or, rather, *didn't* happen last night.'

Flora knew this draw-a-line-in-it attitude should have been a relief, but instead she felt the mortified colour fly to her cheeks. Chances were he'd forgotten last night, not that there was anything to forget. Humiliated, she wished that the floor at her feet would open up to swallow her, or, failing that, that she could think of a flippant comeback line.

'I wish to discuss *why* I am here.'

'I thought that was a state secret, all very "need to know".' The irritable retort came out before she could stop it. 'Sorry!'

'Once more with feeling...?' he suggested drily. 'Has it occurred to you,' he drawled, 'that you're not really cut out for this sort of work?'

'It's not the work, it's—' She stopped herself, but not soon enough to prevent his smug I-told-you-so retort.

'Point proved, I'd say and, as they say, the customer is always right.'

'Or a pain in the—' She bit her lip and forced a stiff smile while continuing to dodge his eyes. 'What can I do for you?'

Next time you feel the urge to insult paying guests, Flora, just think of the accounts, she told herself while she waited for his response. The moment stretched.

'This might be easier if I tell you my full name.'

This conversation, she decided, was getting a bit *Twilight Zone.* Was she meant to recognise him? Did he have some sort of celebrity status, a Hollywood A-lister she was meant to know? He certainly looked the part.

'You mean you signed an alias—you're not Mr Rocco?'

'My name is Ivo Rocco Greco.'

There was a twenty-second time delay before she sat down with a bump, her eyes not leaving his face as she gripped the edge of the table, not even noticing when the tablecloth slipped and sent a jug of milk onto the stone floor.

'Bruno's little brother?' she whispered hoarsely.

He blinked—no one had called him that in a long time—before tipping his dark head in a slow acknowledgement.

Denial lingered; it *still* wasn't sinking in. *'You...?'* she gasped, her voice breathy and faint as her eyes flickered over his lean muscle-toned six-foot-five frame.

He tipped his dark head for a second time in confirmation.

'This is...why on earth didn't you say so earlier?' she exploded, then a moment later, struggling to channel calm, admitted, 'This is just so weird. You're not...'

She was looking embarrassed and anywhere but at him. 'So, Bruno mentioned me?' He felt another stab of fresh guilt. From the day he had decided his brother had deserted him Ivo had never spoken his brother's name again.

She nodded, remembering the underlying protectiveness tinged by guilt in her brother-in-law's face on the occasions he had mentioned his little brother, who it turned out was not at all little. She sighed and said a silent regretful goodbye to the Ivo who had lived in her imagination—a slender, sensitive geek who was the target of bullies.

'I'm not what?'

The soft question brought her eyes up from the menu she was shredding; she dropped the pieces. 'You're…not much like Bruno.'

A good recovery that had the plus of being true.

Her sister's husband had not been above average height, his build slim and wiry, good-looking but not in a jaw-dropping sort of way. Sami said she had fallen in love the moment Bruno smiled… Flora's own smile was sad. Bruno had had a really great smile…and laugh… She fought her way through a wave of sadness.

'You're much…darker.' She shook her head, a furrow appearing across the bridge of her nose. 'I just don't understand why all the secrecy.' Wary suspicion interwoven with the first threads of anger began to emerge from the initial numbing shock that had pushed her brain into basic standby mode. 'And why now?'

It wasn't just that there hadn't been a single member of Bruno's family at the funeral, it was the fact that this brother that Bruno had spoken of with such fondness had never made any attempt to contact him over the years. Now he was here, and the question had to be, why?

Oh, hell, Flora, you're being so slow…he's here for Jamie!

CHAPTER FIVE

IGNORING THE COLD clutch of fear in her stomach, she dealt him a cool, 'over my dead body' glare.

'I thought I made it quite clear to your grandfather's lawyer that I am not about to hand over Jamie. Or,' she challenged, injecting her words with withering scorn, 'are you going to tell me you being here has nothing to do with that at all?'

'I am here on my own behalf.'

Not an exactly comforting statement when made by a man who looked a lot more ruthless than any legal letter—a man who seemed to have inherited the same lack of moral scruples that had been noticeable from her communications with his grandfather.

Her lips twisted into a bitter, contemptuous smile. 'Oh, well, I suppose you could say better late than never. Still, Bruno had plenty of people who *did* care for him and love him to say goodbye—just no one called Greco.'

He responded with a shrug. His expression gave nothing away, certainly not guilt.

'Why didn't you just tell me who you were last

night?' she challenged in an accent thickened by the antagonism that shone in her sea-blue eyes. 'You lied. And save me the semantics—lying by omission is still a lie!' Arms folded across her chest, she lifted her chin and dared him with angry eyes to deny this.

He didn't try, neither did he make any attempt to defend himself, which was a shame because she'd have loved to tell him what she thought about him. She might anyway, she brooded, glaring with dislike at the too-good-looking imposter.

Actually, he seemed content to let her talk, just as he had last night. *And that turned out so well, Flora,* she reminded herself. She had told him things because he was a stranger with no connection to her; she'd revealed weakness, her fears and guilty secrets—*she was a bad mother.*

Would those words cost her—cost Jamie? she wondered. By the time the feelings of vulnerability in her mind translated into words they were angry and directed at the person responsible for her feeling this way.

Flora had never been of the 'don't get mad, get even' school of thought, she just got mad, though she liked to think it wasn't any stereotypical red-headed short fuse. She reserved her ire for people who really deserved it.

And Ivo Greco did!

This brother was as bad *as* his grandfather who had sent her the vile letter via his lawyer. The cold, subtly threatening wording had stayed with her, as had the thoughts of the blood money he had wanted to throw her way.

Hands planted on the table, ignoring the pool of milk and shattered crockery around her feet, fingers clenched into white-knuckled fists, she glared at him, hating the fact that her body hummed with awareness when she looked at him.

'Forget the bill, you're family,' she drawled. Turning away, she tossed her last words over her shoulder. 'But we just closed for the season.'

'I'd say you have another, what, two months before you close permanently.'

Shock froze her to the spot for a moment before, eyes flashing, she spun back, stamped up to the table and glared down at him.

'It may not seem much to you!' she charged, trying hard not to think of the Greco billions and the mountains that that much money could move. The wills it could find loopholes in. 'This place is Jamie's inheritance. I won't let that happen.'

He nodded. 'Good to know. Look, you're annoyed—I get that!'

Her eyes flew wide; this man was unbelievable. *Annoyed!* 'How incredibly *reasonable* of you,' she gritted with teeth-clenching insincerity. 'I'm not annoyed. I'm absolutely furious!'

And it suited her, he decided, allowing his eyes to linger a moment too long on her slightly parted pink lips.

'And don't tell me I've no right to be… *Now,*' she

added with an addition of dark understanding, 'your prowling the house last night makes sense. Were you looking for ammunition to use against me in court? You may have money—' she choked '—but I have right...'

His dark brows lifted, forging a dark bar above his nose as he cut across her in an amused scornful drawl. 'You must be more naive than I thought if you think *right* always wins.'

She felt a chill run down her spine. 'Is that a threat?'

He didn't say a word, just held her eyes, the dark implacability in those still obsidian depths more threat than any words. Flora felt a shudder of visceral fear trace a cold path up her spine and fought against the panic she could feel building. She needed to stay calm and show him she wasn't intimidated... *even if she was!*

'Sorry I didn't oblige you by being drunk in charge of a baby or enjoying an orgy.'

The mental images of a private orgy with the gorgeous fiery redhead delayed his response for several moments. 'It might speed things along if you cut down on the histrionics.'

Her eyes narrowed on his face with dislike. 'You know, your family's sudden interest in Jamie seems just a little bit perverse. You've shown no interest in him before.'

'I didn't know he existed.'

She blinked and tossed out a scornful, 'You expect me to believe that?'

He shrugged, his attitude oozing the sort of arrogant hauteur guaranteed to raise her hackles as he informed her in a bored-sounding drawl, 'You can, and I'm sure will, believe whatever you wish. I have no intention of supplying you with documented proof.'

'You let me tell you about Sami and Bruno and you didn't say anything…' Her voice quivered when she thought about the other things she'd told him, thinking he was a stranger she would never see again. 'It was a cruel thing to do.'

For the first time he looked slightly, not guilty, but, at least, disconcerted, but she held tight to her anger. She had offered an olive branch to Salvatore Greco and got an insult back.

She had to assume Ivo was here because the legal intimidation and bribery hadn't worked. And on that premise, he was the physical equivalent of a legal threat.

She threw up her hands in an attitude of weary disgust and walked stiff-backed across the room before spinning back. Arms folded across her chest, where the tight knot of swirling emotions made her respirations uneven and painful, she fixed him with a tight-lipped glare, finally letting go a soft resigned sigh.

'Fine, say what you have come here to say and just go away.' She adopted an expression of determined uninterest and waited.

'My grandfather is dying.' He watched her uncompromising stance disintegrate as she tumbled from an attitude of righteous indignation to shock, before he saw her expression soften into compassion.

Had the situations been reversed, had Salvatore learnt that the woman who stood between him and what he wanted had been given a death sentence, well, *his* eyes would not be softening with sympathy, that was certain.

'I'm sorry to hear that.'

The thing was they were not just words; he believed her. She was making this too easy and making him feel *guilty*—as if he weren't carrying around enough of that! Her soft-hearted vulnerability was her problem, not his, he reminded himself, and if he took advantage she only had herself to blame.

'Is there much pain?'

He blinked, realising he hadn't asked. 'I don't know. He doesn't...confide.'

She nodded as if she understood, but of course she couldn't. Flora Henderson still believed in the basic goodness of humanity, which was where her greatest vulnerability lay. She had never really accepted that *good* was the exception, the norm was selfishness and avarice and basic 'walk all over your fellow man to claw your way to the top'.

It was inevitable that one day something would wipe the idealistic glow from her beautiful eyes. Ivo was glad that he wouldn't be around to see it...unless he was the catalyst?

'So you came.' Her slender shoulders lifted in enquiry. *'Because?'*

'He wants to see his great-grandson.'

'That was never a problem,' she pointed out. 'He didn't want to see Jamie, he wanted to *buy* him. He wanted me to give up any rights at all. I used to wonder what his family did that was so bad to make Bruno walk away, now I know.' But *this* man hadn't walked away; he was one of them. A fact that, for Jamie's sake, she couldn't allow herself to forget.

'Sami and Bruno wanted me to...' Her eyes fell, then lifted, blazing with defiance as they fixed on his face, daring him to throw last night's admission back at her as she said in a voice that shook with sincerity, 'I may not be the world's best mother, but I love Jamie, and I'm not about to hand him over for any amount of money. I'm sorry your grandfather is ill but it's not going to happen.'

Dio. Fair play seemed to be this woman's middle name, so why the hell did he feel so bad about using this to his own advantage?

'Sure, I get that.'

Her eyes widened before fluttering in confusion. 'You do?'

His gaze moved around the room before it landed on her face. 'This place means a lot to you?'

'They built it...for Jamie.'

The quiver in her voice made his jaw clench. 'Is it the life you wanted?'

She gave him a blank look and shook her head, looking at him as though he were talking a foreign language.

'You're what? Twenty-five? Twenty-six?' He was genuinely curious; had it ever crossed her mind to refuse the burden that had been gifted her?

'You tell me, you seem to know everything,' she retorted snappily. 'I suppose you have some creepy file on my life.'

He shrugged, the smile that lifted the corners of his mouth mocking. 'It's a very thin file.' He demonstrated the point by extending his hand, holding his thumb and forefinger almost touching and watched her eyes widen with horror.

'I wasn't being serious!' she squeaked.

Welcome to my world, he thought. It was one she wouldn't fit into. 'Don't worry, there was nothing Salvatore could use for leverage, or he already would have.'

He sounded so chillingly casual that all Flora could do was stare.

'I didn't come here to blackmail you or bribe you or propose…'

'What?'

'My grandfather's favoured option is we marry, and somewhere down the line divorce, at which point I will gain full custody of Jamie.'

Her laugh was the result of nerves, not any appreciation of the joke. 'You're not *serious*?'

'*I'm* not.' But you had to hand it to Salvatore, there was a certain attractive simplicity to the plan. Not that he had for one moment considered the proposition any more than he would have considered allowing a vulnerable baby to be moulded into adulthood by Salvatore. His lips twisted into a self-derisory grimace as his glance flickered downward over himself. *Look how well you turned out!*

Her teeth clenched as she watched one corner of his mouth twitch into a lazy half-smile. 'Sorry, the *amusing* part has just passed me by. Care to share?' she tossed out sarcastically.

'Would it hurt to go along with a dying man's last wishes?' he asked, watching through the skein of his lashes as uncertainty swamped the anger in her blue eyes; followed a moment later by compassion, just as he'd known it would be.

Damping an inconvenient stab of conscience, he reminded himself that it was not his task to protect her from her own kind heart, it was hers to toughen up. The alternative was going through life being used—he wasn't the only unscrupulous bastard out there.

It had been obvious to him within five minutes of meeting her that one of Flora Henderson's flaws was that she would always do the *right* thing, even if that right thing made her miserable. She possessed the thing that made her one of life's victims—a tender heart!

He knew that she would not hesitate to sacrifice her own happiness if it was the *right* thing to do. All he had to do was convince her it was the right thing and he really didn't think it would take an awful lot of effort on his part. Not once he actually got her back to Italy—the rest was inevitable. Once she saw the sort of life the baby could have being brought up as a Greco, the sort of advantages that he could give the child, she wouldn't be able to help herself doing the right thing.

'Obviously, I'm sorry.'

He arched a brow. 'Really? You're not just a tiniest bit glad?'

Insulted by the suggestion, she stared stonily back at him.

'You're going to lose this place, you know.'

She clamped her mouth closed over a denial that she knew would be a lie.

'And then what will happen—you both move in with your mother?' He arched a brow and watched her face. 'You've thought of that, but I suppose you're also thinking she's not getting any younger, and she's already brought up her children. She needs a rest, but what option will you have? And, of course, there is no work here for an up-and-coming architect so you'll move back to Edinburgh or Glasgow?'

She fought the urge to cover her ears and shut out the horribly insidious voice putting her worst unacknowledged fears into words. 'I've not thought—'

'That far ahead?' he inserted smoothly. 'I get that, but you're going to have to when you stop thinking some sort of miracle is going to happen. Will you take Jamie with you and farm him out to a nursery?' he pressed, as he relentlessly continued to paint a picture of the future that Flora didn't want to see.

'Or leave him here with your mother? Do you think that your sister and Bruno would want any of that for their son? Do you think that was what they had in mind when they made you his guardian?'

'My mum is too old to…' Biting her lip as she felt the press of tears behind her eyes, she shook her head. 'You don't know what is best for Jamie.'

'Do you?'

Unable to respond, she turned her head away, closing her eyes to shut out his dark, relentless stare.

He saw the doubts in her face and pressed home his advantage, reminding the guilty whisper in his head that nothing he was saying was not the truth. 'How hard do you think that it will be a few months down the line, after you're late a few times to pick up the baby from nursery, or get the sack because you take too much time off when the baby is sick? How hard will it be then to convince a court that I'd be a better guardian?'

'There is such a thing as employment law and State help. Working single parents cope—'

Each word was a direct hit at his pride, but when she said cope as though that were a good thing, he couldn't hold his outrage in. He surged to his feet, swearing under his breath; the fact that she took an involuntary step back only increased his outrage. What the hell did she think he was going to do?

'I do not want my nephew to *cope*! He is a Greco, he will not *cope* on government handouts and *charity*!'

Wow...when he shrugged off urbane and reasonable he did it big time! '*Half* a Greco.'

The provocation earned her a killer glare.

'And if you think you can intimidate me—'

'I'm not trying to intimidate you!'

She let out a weak laugh; if this was him *not* trying, she wouldn't like to see him put any effort in.

'Has it occurred to you that I might be the miracle you are waiting for?' he remarked in a conversational tone.

'I do not think miracle when I look at you.'

He sketched a quick smile. 'I'm being serious.'

She viewed the change of tack with deep suspicion and rolled her eyes. 'Oh, and I suppose you want me to keep Jamie.'

He shook his head in a negative motion. 'I think you could be Aunt Flora who Jamie has holidays with on Skye and who gives him nice birthday presents.'

'Well, at least you're honest.'

In this instance honesty worked, but that didn't mean he wouldn't have lied through his teeth if it suited him in order to achieve what he wanted.

He nodded. 'I may disagree with Salvatore's methods but I do believe that Jamie should be brought up in Italy. I came here to offer a compromise of sorts that would mean your financial problems are over and my grandfather will die a happy man.' For Salvatore, happy meant getting his own way.

Flora didn't relax. She reminded herself that *this*

brother hadn't rejected his heritage, his position of privilege; he was as dangerous as the grandfather.

'Unless of course you're not interested in Jamie's future.'

Her chin went up at the suggestion as she glared at him through narrowed eyes. 'Jamie's future is here.'

'Here or a bedsit in Edinburgh with no garden and noisy neighbours. And what sort of schooling would he receive? You would really deprive Jamie of everything I can give him?'

Nothing he said was wrong or even exaggerated. Flora pushed down the choking tide of panic she could feel building.

'You have a problem; I have a solution. One that isn't marry me and live unhappily ever after.'

She gave a tense nod and thought, *I'm probably going to regret this.* 'I'm listening.'

'I suggest you and Jamie come back to Italy with me—think of it as a holiday.'

'To Italy! What would that solve? Anyway,' she said, shaking her head from side to side, 'I'm not going anywhere with you.'

He dug a hand into his pocket, catching the velvet pouch that held the ring in his fingers. 'How about you hear me out?'

She responded to the sardonic request with a slow reluctant nod of her head.

'Come back to Italy with me as my fiancée.'

For at least ten seconds she managed to keep her mouth shut, until the pressure of the low heavy thud in her head got too much to resist. 'An interesting suggestion, which, in case you were wondering, is a polite way of say you're insane. Utterly mad!' she croaked with deep conviction.

'Calm down!'

'I'm perfectly calm.' The strange thing was she actually was. Her heart had slowed to a low, regular thud.

His lips twisted into a smile. She made him think of a spooked horse ready to run for the hills. One false word or move and she'd be gone.

'I have no wish to be married, though I would like to know my brother's child and have him know his heritage. He will one day inherit a great deal.'

'Jamie will…?'

'Of course, hadn't that occurred to you?'

She shook her head, recalling a couple of comments her sister had made…but seriously rich? Bruno had been so normal, his brother was not. It was not difficult to imagine this man occupying the weird world of the *uber*-rich—he was a man who made his own rules.

'My grandfather is too old to change and I see no reason he shouldn't die a happy man. Let him *think* we're getting married.'

'What on earth made him think I'd agree to marry you, that we'd…' her eyes fell as she felt a flush of embarrassment wash over her skin before tacking on an awkward '…*fall in love*?'

'He cares little about the how—it is a means to

an end. And you can relax, my grandfather knows that I do not fall in love.'

The air of utter confidence he delivered this statement with, as if it were a fact as indisputable as the chemical formula of water, dragged a strangled laugh from Flora's throat, as for a brief moment her sense of humour reasserted itself.

'Sorry, you just sounded so ridiculous…' Her voice trailed off. She was guessing from his expression that he had little experience of being called ridiculous. 'Well, I suppose it is good to know I won't be expected to act loved up for his benefit.'

What did she look like *loved up*? he wondered, seeing those pink lips parted and swollen from kisses. The blue eyes glazed with passion. The effort of ignoring the flash of scalding, body-hardening heat gave his voice a throaty, abrasive quality as he explained.

'Salvatore is only interested in the parental rights marriage brings, not the merging of souls.' He tilted his head a little as he studied her face. 'Was that a yes…?'

The acrid mockery in his statement made her wince. 'Not even a maybe.' Though it was and they both knew it. The knowledge, the lack of alternatives, felt like walls closing in around her.

'Look, the deal I'm suggesting is come out with me, pretend to be my fiancée. Let Salvatore meet his great-grandson and for that I will clear the debts on this place, which will give the option of staying on or selling it as a profitable going concern. The alternative, we both know, is foreclosure.'

His fingers interwoven, he watched her, the internal struggle being waged in her head visible in the expressive, fine-boned face.

'What will I tell people…my mother?' She reacted to the flicker in his hooded eyes and added quickly, 'Not that I'm agreeing to anything.'

'That is, *would* be, up to you.' His smile said he knew as well as she did that she was just playing for time. 'The truth or maybe a version of it that suits you.'

'You're probably better than me with versions of the truth.'

'My grandfather's dying wish is to see his great-grandson and you are taking Jamie out there—surely she would understand that? You need a holiday, some sun.'

He was right, her mum would accept that. She began to feel panicky as her legitimate reasons to resist continued to vanish.

'As for the financial problems resolving—'

'She doesn't know… Nobody—' Her long lashes lifted and he was on the receiving end of the full resentful glare of her cerulean-blue eyes. 'I *thought* nobody knew.'

'It never crossed your mind to ask for help?' Stupid question, he realised—she was too stubborn and independent to ask for a sticking plaster if she was bleeding out! 'Has anyone ever mentioned the downsides of sticking your head in the sand?'

The sarcasm brought an angry flush to her cheeks. 'If I did go along with this, this…*arrangement*…' not a bad word for insanity '… I'd need some guarantees,' she said, resisting the feeling that she was just being swept along.

He arched a sable brow. 'Such as?'

'I will need my own…space.'

His mouth quirked. '*Space* is not a problem, but you're not talking about space, are you, *cara*?' he drawled, his smile deepening as she flushed like some sort of virgin. 'You're talking about beds. You will have your own private suite, and rest assured I never enter a lady's room without an invitation.'

There would be no shortage of those coming his way, she thought with a scowl. 'Like a vampire.' There was nothing even vaguely undead about his vibrant colouring. Flora found the vitality he oozed exhausting at close quarters.

'A creature of the night, hmm?' he drawled, rubbing his chin. 'I've been called worse.'

'Of that,' she retorted tartly, 'I have no doubt.'

'So, any other demands?'

'I'd say common courtesy but I'm a realist.'

His deep, warm, appreciative chuckle tickled her nerve endings in a not entirely unpleasant way.

'So when I decide to return home there will be no attempt to prevent me…*and* Jamie.'

'*Your* decision every step of the way.'

She frowned, for some reason worried about how easy he was making this. 'I suppose…'

'So that's a yes, then, you agree.'

'But how—?'

His voice, implacably cool, cut across her protests. 'Agree or not? Leave the how to me.'

'I agree,' she said, turning a deaf ear to the voice in her head that said she had just signed away her soul for security.

CHAPTER SIX

IF HE HAD shown any hint of smug complacency she would, Flora decided, have slapped him.

But he didn't. There was zero reaction on his lean, dark face as, without missing a beat, he angled a speculative brow and said, 'How does forty-eight hours sound?'

Her hands, which had been clenched into fists, relaxed but she was mystified by his question. 'Sound for what?'

He gave a sardonic smile. 'To organise things this end.'

Her eyes flew wide, her lashes fluttering like trapped butterflies against her cheek. 'So soon? But I thought that...'

'I'd give you time to change your mind?'

Her lips tightened. 'I agreed!'

'And your word is your bond. Good to know. However, the situation is somewhat urgent. Salvatore is dying.'

The obvious response to this reminder was—when?

He couldn't see the thought but he could see the

guilt that followed in its wake move across her transparent face.

This was a woman who should never play poker.

Her being too nice to press the issue worked well for him because the truth was he didn't know. The truth was Ivo would be more shocked to learn that his grandfather was really dying than if it turned out to be another of his imaginative manipulations.

His factory setting was extreme scepticism where Salvatore was concerned, but he would deal with any surprises once he got Flora and Jamie to Italy.

'Look, I've got some things to keep me busy in London—you just organise you and the baby and I'll be back for you.'

He made it sound ludicrously simple, as if you could just walk away from your life and it would be waiting for you when you returned. 'But this place.' With a shake of her head she looked around the room. 'The bookings We have an arrangement with local artists and artisans...'

'Yes, I'd noticed. Good marketing. Symbiotic. I'll buy everything—how will that work?'

She blinked at the casual way he said it. 'That sculpture over there.' She nodded towards the window embrasure where a stone carved otter stood.

He nodded. 'Nice.'

'And expensive. Neil has five more works displayed around the place.' The local sculptor had some of his larger pieces of work displayed in government buildings.

'It looks good there.'

'So is that your plan? If there's a problem throw money at it.'

'Do you have a problem with that?'

She lowered her eyes, knowing that if she said yes she could be accused of hypocrisy—after all, she wasn't complaining about the money he was throwing at her.

'Just so long as you know.'

'Fine, then just email me the details and I'll arrange refunds and throw in an expenses-paid break later in the year. I can't see many people complaining.'

He was knocking down her objections like skittles before she even had a chance to line them up. Before she had a chance to think through the implications of what desperation had led her to so recklessly agree to.

The desperation hadn't gone away, she reminded herself.

Could he genuinely not see problems or was he just ignoring them? she wondered, her frustration growing at his leave-it-to-me attitude. She didn't like leaving it to anyone. Flora took responsibility for her own decisions. 'But how are we going to explain closing?'

His broad shoulders lifted in a negligent elegant shrug. 'A full refurbishment?'

'We don't need refurbishing!' she protested indignantly.

'I'll think of something, don't worry.'

She bridled at the verbal-pat-on-the-head attitude; she could almost see him moving on in his head. Well, no one could accuse him of letting the grass grow, that was for sure!

'Right, I'll be back Friday.' Moving towards the door, he turned back. 'I almost forgot.'

He strode back towards her. Unprepared for the action, she didn't resist, and he caught her wrist, turned her hand over and one by one curled her clenched fingers open to reveal her palm.

Flora was conscious of a strange, breathless sensation as she looked at his brown fingers against her own. The breath caught in her chest escaped in a long, slow, sibilant breath when he tipped up a velvet pouch and a ring landed in her palm.

Her eyes lifted to the lean dark face of the man bent over her hand. 'What's that?' she asked, her voice a throaty whisper.

It invited a sarcastic comeback but he didn't accept the invitation.

Ivo took hold of the ring and slid it onto her extended finger. 'Believe you me, *cara*, this is something I never thought I'd be doing.' Never wanted to, and yet even though his feelings were not involved, the symbolism—yes, it had to be the symbolism—made things shift inside him. 'I suppose I should be looking to you for guidance?' Why should the thought of another man putting a ring on this finger make him feel so…? Not jealous, that would have been absurd, but he just felt angry because she hadn't seen her ex for the loser he clearly was.

She stared from the finger that held a gleaming diamond to Ivo's face for a moment and back; her confusion was not feigned. For a moment she had no idea what he was talking about and then she realised… Callum!

She clenched her fingers and pulled her hand back. The ring glittered against her skin.

It wasn't as if she had forgotten, or the moment hadn't seemed special at the time, but quite crazily she remembered nothing approaching this heart-pounding shock, even though Callum had proposed prettily.

Callum's proposal had been like a well-rehearsed and smoothly stage-managed love scene in a play. And yet, perfect hadn't made her feel dizzy, just self-conscious and slightly nervous that she'd miss her cue and say the wrong thing to spoil the *prettiness*.

The irony was, Callum had been pretending. Ivo wasn't pretending he was giving her anything other than a prop; he didn't *do* love.

Then the disturbing realisation hit her, granted what she was feeling had nothing to do with love… *couldn't* have anything to do with love. No, this was about chemical attraction, and the attraction she felt for Ivo was a billion times stronger than anything she had felt for her ex-fiancé!

'So, do you always carry around a chunk of diamond in your pocket?'

'I like to be prepared.'

'Perhaps I should proofread this file? You might have got some things wrong,' she snapped waspishly.

'Oh, if you have trouble sleeping I'd recommend it.'

'I suppose your life is fascinating.'

'You're about to find out, *cara*.'

He watched her expression change as the reality came crashing in. 'You'll be ready to leave.'

It wasn't a suggestion and Flora couldn't let the order—*any* order—pass unchallenged. You gave in to an arrogant man drunk on his own power and self-importance once and he'd walk all over you—helped in no small part by her hormones, unless she took control!

She was no longer that silly romantic girl, but maybe a lustful woman was more dangerous?

'Thursday suits me better.' But it didn't, did it? It didn't suit her at all.

The moment the words left her lips, Flora wished them unsaid, but, the damage done, she fought to keep the dismay from showing. She'd established she was no pushover but that token gesture had given her one day *less* to prepare—unless he was difficult, in which case she could concede with dignity.

Please be difficult!

He studied her, a flicker of a smile moving across his face, though when he responded it was with perfect solemnity. 'Absolutely, whatever you say, *cara*.'

* * *

Flora took Jamie to say goodbye to her mum, leaving herself plenty of time to be back in the time that Ivo had said he'd arrive.

Flora, feeling guilty as hell for lying to her mother, had gone for the partial-truth option.

When Flora had explained the situation her mum, being family orientated herself, had agreed that of course Flora must take Jamie to meet his Italian family, even though she would obviously miss her grandson but, as her sister was coming to visit from Australia, she wouldn't be lonely.

It wasn't until Flora was making her last farewells that she realised she might have spoken more than she realised about Ivo Greco.

'I know you were hurt, Flora,' her mum said quietly, 'by that wee idiot, Callum, but not all men are alike.'

Startled, Flora finished strapping Jamie in his car seat and turned back, one hand on the door.

'I'm not, Mum. What made you say that?'

'The way you were talking about Bruno's little brother.'

Flora hurriedly did a mental review of their conversation. Had she been talking about him...*that* much? 'Oh, Mum, he's not little. He's—'

'Fair enough, and it's true I've never met the man, but in my experience there is a big difference between an *arrogant* man who loves the sound of his own voice and can't stop boring you with how marvellous he is, and a man who is quietly confident and listens to your opinion.' Balanced on the one crutch she had been promoted to, she hugged her daughter.

Some people listened to music when they drove, some people liked company. Ivo liked neither. He enjoyed the solitude of driving, the fact that he could legitimately ignore an email or phone, and call it being a considerate law-abiding driver.

If he'd actually been travelling with the woman he was to marry he supposed that he might have felt obliged to make conversation, but he wasn't.

Basic civility required that he respond if she spoke but he had no intention of encouraging conversation, and definitely not initiating it!

The baby had fallen asleep almost the instant he'd been strapped into his baby seat in the back, and Flora had been totally silent.

There was more than one sort of silence.

This one was not relaxing. He recognised the perversity of his reaction when he even started feeling irritated by the fact she seemed to feel no need to break it.

'Are you all right?'

Flora started, her head whipped around his way, the fat, shiny plait she had her hair confined in today landing with a *thunk* on her shoulder. 'Yes.' She glanced at the baby in the back, before training her eyes once more on the side window, wrapped up in her own thoughts.

He let the monosyllable lie another ten minutes before the compulsion to prod her into a response overcame him. It was not about hearing her voice, although the light accent was pleasing on the ear.

'Babies don't travel light.' The boot of the car was capacious but it was full to the brim of clutter that was apparently essential for babies. Loading it in had been like a military operation. There had barely been room for the small bag that Flora had brought—either she did travel light, which would make her a very unusual woman in his experience, or she wasn't expecting to be staying long.

'No.' This time she didn't even turn her head.

His jaw clenched as the conviction the silent treatment was deliberate grew.

He didn't speak again until they had passed a sign that said the airport was another ten miles. They'd made good time. 'I'm beginning to think you're ignoring me, *cara*?'

Flora almost laughed...*ignore*!

As if there were any way in the world she could have ignored six feet five of vital masculinity in this enclosed space. Air-conditioning or not, she could feel the warmth of his skin and smell the warm clean male scent of his body. The combination did not make for a relaxing journey.

'You usually have a lot to say for yourself.'

Callum had once said something similar, accusing her after a meeting with friends that she had hogged the conversation. The irony hadn't struck her until later that Callum liked talking about himself so much that she rarely got to contribute to any conversation. She didn't have to. He enjoyed worshipful silence.

And she'd been stupid enough to supply it!

Her eyes slid to her travelling companion. While Ivo Greco's arrogance entered a room before he did, he could not be accused of bragging, but her mum was wrong. The fact that any personal information had to be dragged out of him didn't mean he couldn't have taught lessons in arrogance.

'I was thinking, wondering, if I'm not doing the most stupid thing I've ever done in my life.' She'd also been trying to figure out a way of asking how long her stay was likely to be without making it sound as if she were wishing for his grandfather's death.

So far she hadn't come up with one.

His brows lifted. 'I suppose, *cara*, it depends how stupid the most stupid thing you've done previously was.'

Her lips moved in a whisper of a smile, which vanished like smoke as she admitted ruefully, 'It was pretty stupid.' Falling for Callum was stupid. Believing he'd loved her was even more stupid.

A bit of hero worship, at fifteen, was one thing. She wasn't the only local girl who'd had the local boy who'd become an international football legend on her bedroom wall. She wasn't the only one to compete for a glimpse of him on his rare visits home to see his parents who still lived in the house he'd grown up in.

But she *was* the only one who had bumped into the sporting hero a few years later in Edinburgh. She'd been flattered when he'd recognised her and in a state of disbelief when he had invited her to dinner.

One short month later he'd proposed. Walking on air, she'd accepted, but even before she'd had a chance to share the news, it had been over. At least the humiliation had been private.

Her gaze flickered to the man beside her. How many hearts had he broken? she wondered. Did he keep count? she mused cynically. Did he even remember their names?

A pothole in the road that jolted her made her realise how long she'd been staring at him, in a way that could, to the casual observer, be confused with drooling. Ashamed and a little alarmed at the conscious effort it required to drag her gaze from his patrician profile, she rubbed the ring finger on her left hand hard.

It was only at the last minute that she had remembered to take off the ring Ivo had produced and slipped onto her finger before he'd left. She'd just managed to stuff it in her handbag before her mum had appeared from the pottery.

Handbag! She experienced a flurry of panic... hadn't she?

The noise of Flora scrabbling in her handbag drew his attention sideways for long enough to register the panic on her face.

'What's wrong?'

Heart thudding with trepidation, Flora shook her head and dumped the entire contents of her handbag onto her knee.

'The ring…was…is it real?' She aimed for casual and produced shrill panic.

'You mean is it fictitious?'

Irritated, she cut across him. 'I mean, is it a real diamond?'

He arched a brow. 'You're worried I'd fob you off with a fake?' He shook his head in an attitude of mock hurt. 'You think I'm cheap.'

'I think you're…' She inhaled a deep relieved breath and sank back weakly in her seat as her fingers closed around an object that had slipped into a hole in the bag lining. A moment later it was in her shaking hand. 'Thank God!' she breathed in fervent relief as she slipped the rock onto her finger.

'It fits well.'

'Yes, but I'd feel a lot happier if it was in a bank vault,' she said darkly.

'It looks better on your finger.'

Flora, who was repacking the collection of female essentials that had spilled onto her lap, turned her head. 'I thought I'd lost it. I nearly had heart failure.'

'It's just a ring.'

'Oh!' An explanation for his relaxed attitude occurred to her. 'Is it insured?'

'I hadn't got around to that.'

The pucker between her feathery brows that had been sitting there all morning deepened as she remembered her mother's comments. She was not ready to admit that there wasn't any commonality between the two of them, but on the subject of expensive rings the two reacted *very* differently.

Callum had had no hesitation accepting the ring that she had slid off her trembling finger after he'd dumped her. She could still hear the moral indignation in his voice as he'd accused her of tricking him, of hiding the truth from him.

'I mean, kids, a family, what other reason does a guy get *married* for?'

'Oh, I don't know—love?'

He'd laughed, actually *laughed* at her then, explaining the way you did to a small child or someone not very bright, 'There are plenty of girls out there for love. A wife is different—a man puts her on a pedestal.'

She didn't know about the pedestal but he had put the woman he had married two months after he'd dumped Flora in a mansion, several, actually, and, just as he'd said, there were still plenty of girls out there giving Callum love...or at least *sex*. Callum had never had any intention of changing his lifestyle for something like marriage...he believed he could have it all, and he did.

The wife *had* to know about the girlfriends. It wasn't as if Callum was discreet, and there were always cameras and phones around to record any social-media-worthy action of an ex-premier-league footballer, but did the beautiful blonde know that the ring she wore had once been on someone else's finger? Flora wondered, staring down at the diamond glittering on her own finger.

She had been devastated at the time but Flora appreciated now that she'd had a lucky escape. She only wished it was good judgement and not a biological failing on her part that was responsible.

'Stop worrying.'

Her eyes lifted and made fleeting contact with Ivo's dark stare. *He can't read your mind,* she soothed herself, managing a huff of scornful laughter.

'Easy for you to say!'

At the wheel Ivo stiffened in response to being snapped at. The women in his life purred and smiled, and the novelty value of having this redhead snarl up at him had limited novelty value. Before he could react in kind there was a grumpy snuffling sound from the back seat, followed by a wail.

'See what you've done now,' she reproached, ignoring his indignant growl of, *'Me!'* as she twisted around in her seat and murmured soothingly, 'Hush, Jamie, we're nearly there.'

Actually, they were there.

It took seconds for him to park up in the small terminal.

There was no struggling with bags this end; what appeared to be an army of people arrived and began to unpack the luggage. Their progress through customs was equally swift and effortless and it felt like moments later that they were on the plane with no airline logo, though inside Greco was discreetly evident from the headed notepaper to the coasters on the table.

Ivo told her to make herself at home and vanished, leaving her to cope with the baby. She'd have liked to call him selfish but there were several hovering staff offering her assistance.

Having read up on travelling by air with a baby, Flora spent take-off and the next part of the journey feeding Jamie, who didn't appear to suffer any problems with the change in pressure. She had just got him changed and back to sleep when Ivo appeared.

He wasn't alone.

'This is Cristina.' The young woman smiled. 'She's one of the nannies.'

It would have made less sense to Flora if he had said the woman was part of a boy band. 'What do you mean, *the nannies*?' The plural part hadn't passed her by.

'Well, Nanny Emily is getting on, though don't let her hear me say it.' The young woman beside him smiled. 'And—'

Flora cut him off mid-sentence. 'If you think I'm handing Jamie over to anyone, you are off your head!'

After scanning her angry face, Ivo turned to the young woman and said something in Italian that made her vanish. 'I'm trying to make your life easier here,' he said, struggling to hang onto his temper.

Flora flung back the plait, and shook her head, causing stray red curls to drift across her face. Ivo, distracted by those golden-tinted wisps, fought a strong compulsion to push them back.

'No, you are trying to take over my life. Jamie's life.' Give him an inch and she'd be asking his permission before she decided what dress to wear. This man was so typical of the breed, she decided, forgetting she had ever imagined for one second that she had misjudged him.

'Where is the harm in having a nanny?' Not accustomed to considering anyone's convenience but his own, Ivo had rationalised the efforts he had made to make the journey and stay as comfortable and stress-free for Flora as possible by telling himself it had nothing whatever to do with sentiment, it was simple practicality.

The last thing he wanted was her gratitude. He just wanted Jamie. Admittedly they came as a package but *that*, he hoped, was a temporary situation.

Not gratitude, but the last thing he had *expected* was her spitting fury!

Flora compressed her lips. 'No harm at all if you live in the nineteenth century,' she agreed with a smile that aimed for provocation, and if the tightening of the muscles around his mouth was any indication she succeeded.

'Ever heard of delegation?'

'Ever heard of consultation?' she retorted, planting her hands on her hips as her chin lifted another defiant notch. 'Ground rules, Ivo, where Jamie is concerned I make the decisions. Is that clear?'

The look of astonishment that flickered across his incredibly handsome face might have been funny in other, less fraught, circumstances.

'Was that an *ultimatum*?' he grated, clinging to his temper.

'Excellent,' she approved. 'You're catching on. It's possible you're not as stupid as you look.' About halfway through she sort of knew she'd gone too far, but she was on a roll and couldn't stop. She knew she was shaking; it was always that way when she let her anger get the better of her.

He didn't say a word, he just looked down at her. The colour that had flamed in her face had faded, leaving it washed pale; her eyes were blue pools, the defiance in them now tinged with wariness. With no warning his anger snuffed out.

She looked so tired but she was so stubborn. In his head an image materialised of him holding her until the stiff rigidity in her shoulders dissolved, she dissolved against him, warm and... He gave his head a sharp jarring shake to dislodge the image and the emotions that went with it.

'I was trying to help, but if you enjoy being in a state of permanent exhaustion—fine!' he said, wrapping up his misplaced concern in irritation. 'Your choice. But for God's sake sit down before you fall down!'

Flora did, not because she was grateful for his reminder that she looked awful, but because her knees were shaking in reaction to the emotional confronta-

tion. *Probably the first of many, Flora girl, so you
need to toughen up.*

'I should have discussed it with you.'

The concession made her eyes widen.

'But I just assumed...'

'What, that babies have an army of nannies and
live in nurseries?'

'I did,' he said.

'And look how well that turned out!'

He responded to her soft taunt with a grin that
literally took her breath away. Wow, if Ivo Greco
decided to seduce a girl she'd be seduced, Flora realised, no if, but or even maybe.

In her anxiety to push away the thoughts and the
insidious warmth unfurling low in her belly and confusing rush of feeling that came with it, she said the
first thing that came into her head, a question that was
already there but she'd never intended actually to ask.

'How old were you when your parents died?'

His smile vanished to be replaced by a more familiar hauteur. She bent her head, waiting; she could
almost *smell* the chilly put-down coming her way.

It didn't come.

'I was a few months old when my mother died.'
Her head came up with a snap. 'She was diagnosed
with breast cancer when she was pregnant, but she
delayed treatment until after I was born... So you
could say I killed her.'

His father had.

He'd apologised the next day, tears streaming

down his face as he'd said over and over, *'I didn't mean it.'*

It was not a memory he accessed voluntarily, though the smell of stale alcohol on someone's breath always brought the moment back.

'Only if you were a total idiot!' she retorted, hotly indignant—furious! Surely *no one* would allow a child to think that? To potentially carry that sort of guilt through life and into adulthood?

Eyes misted, she turned her head sharply, embarrassed by the emotions that threatened to find release in tears, emotions that only intensified as her eyes drifted towards the figure of the sleeping baby.

She might never know what it felt like to hold her own baby but she could imagine—imagine being willing to give anything for the life you had created.

'I remember my dad,' she said to fill the silence that was growing. 'Though it's hard to know when the memories are mine and when they are stories mum and Sami told me, if you know what I mean.'

'Our father didn't tell us stories. He drank and he wept, spent weeks in bed and then he killed himself because he couldn't live without her.' *And you are telling her this* why, *Ivo?*

The fact that this tragic information was delivered in a tone that was totally devoid of any emotion made it all the more shocking.

Flora's tender heart ached in her chest; she hurt for the boy he'd been, the pain real.

'Poor man,' she whispered, thinking of poor boys

left to be brought up by an army of nannies and a grandfather who, if the Internet opinion of him was even half true, was not exactly warm and cuddly. Flora was *really* trying hard to reserve judgement, but it wasn't easy.

'Poor man...' Ivo ground out the words as he surged to his feet.

Flora sat still and silent. His intimidating height advantage was emphasised even more than normal by the confined environment. 'I just meant—'

'*Weak* man,' he bit back in a clear, cold, contemptuous voice before dark lashes veiled the anger and pain she had glimpsed in his eyes and he delivered the abrupt addition. 'To allow a child to find him—' He stopped, an arrested expression stealing across his face as if he had just realised what he had said.

'You...*you* found him?'

His face was wiped clean of all emotion as he met her tear-filled gaze; everything inside him rejected the one thing he hated above all else: pity. 'I have work. Anything you want...'

And he was gone, striding into the next compartment of the private jet, leaving Flora wondering about the revealing moment and the little boy scared by seeing something no child should.

CHAPTER SEVEN

'WOULD AN OFFER of help get my head bitten off?'
Ivo was all for self-sufficiency, but she took it into
the realm of the ridiculous.

Flora, who hadn't heard him come up behind her
as she tucked the baby into his buggy and adjusted
his sun hat, gave a startled jump at the sound of his
voice at her shoulder.

She didn't realise how disturbingly close he was
until she straightened up and half turned, finding
they were standing almost touching. The sensation
that made her head spin sizzled along her nerve endings and sent her stomach into a violent dip.

Her eyes made the slow journey from mid-chest
level up to his lean, dark face. There was no trace of
the emotions that had blazed earlier in his enigmatic
stare; his expression was inscrutable.

But now she had glimpsed past the mask she
couldn't help but wonder what else his impregnable
shell of control hid besides a toxic relationship with
his late father.

None of your business, Flora girl. He's not your

business. The romance is fake. It's not your job to understand him or heal him. He'd laugh in your face at the idea he needs healing.

And maybe, she mused, he was right.

His voice cut across her internal dialogue.

'Well, are you?'

She looked at him blankly. 'Nervous?'

It wasn't what he'd asked and if he was honest not something he had even considered. The acknowledgement came with a stab of guilt tinged with irritation. He didn't need to change. He didn't want to change. Any changing and compromise would be hers to do. *Dio*, why the hell did she have to be so in touch with her feelings about everything anyway? he wondered, ignoring the fact that it was this aspect of her personality—the soft heart, the desire to put the needs of others above her own—that he was relying on to deliver his nephew into his care.

Flora shrugged and dodged his dark brooding stare. If she hadn't been nervous she was now, and not only of what waited outside.

The earlier conversation had made her think of him in a new light, not as a man who was invulnerable but someone who might actually have some weak spots. Just when she had got comfortable with thinking of him as a man who was one of life's takers, a Callum, a man she could comfortably dismiss, a man she wouldn't allow herself to be attracted to.

'A bit.'

He took a half-step back and she almost wept, so

intense was her relief to put a few more inches of air between them. She had to ask herself whether the problem lay with him or her... No, actually, she didn't have to ask herself anything—and she wouldn't.

Resurrecting a little defiance, albeit a slightly less focused version, she lifted a hand to her face and absently brushed a curl from her cheek. The braid in her hair was unravelling as fast as she was!

'Do I have time to freshen up?'

His heavy-lidded gaze slid over the soft curves of her face, lingering a second or two too long on the plump fullness of her lips before he ventured a response. 'You look fine to me, but if you need—'

Flustered by the way he was looking at her, she shook her head. 'No. I'm fine.'

He watched through his half-lowered lids as she tweaked the baby's cap, even though it didn't need tweaking. She looked, he decided, better than fine.

A lot better!

He recognised the compulsive element as his glance slid over her slim figure, but he didn't have an appetite to fight it.

He *liked* looking at her. It was a weakness he was ready to admit to and looking at her was infinitely preferable to having her loose in his head, even if he had invited the invasion by revealing far too much. He still didn't know what madness had possessed him to make him open up that way.

During the flight, while he'd renewed his acquaintance with the pilot, he'd tried and failed to analyse why she acted as some sort of catalyst to feelings he had buried—best thing for them—and failed.

He'd settled for a slightly unsatisfactory verdict: that it wouldn't be happening again, but he could carry on looking.

And where was the harm?

Except to his blood pressure.

Today her hair was tied again, though in a looser plait affair that left curls trailing down her neck and around her face. She had opted to wear a shift dress with a swirly pattern of soft blues and greens that showed off her slim arms and incredible legs. Looking at the slim calves reminded him of the only other time he'd seen her legs. The memory of the sizzling tension of that night still retained enough residual heat to make his skin prickle and his gut tighten.

'Are you going to accept some help?'

She straightened up gracefully and did the flip thing with her hair. Every time she did it he thought about unwinding that plait and spreading the hair… 'Help,' he exclaimed abruptly.

In response to her bemused expression, Ivo nodded at the stroller where Jamie was doing his impression of a perfect baby, kicking his legs and looking cute and smiley. 'Do you want to negotiate the steps or…?' He arched a satiric brow and added drily, 'In case you were wondering, this is me discussing it with you.'

Flora decided to ignore the sarcasm. Instead she

nodded to the two uniformed figures waiting to carry the buggy down the steps.

'Thanks so much.'

Ivo watched the men melt as she smiled at them.

Behind her Flora heard Ivo swear; it was an impressive bilingual effort. She half turned to look at him as the men hoisted the buggy between them, a questioning frown painting furrows in her wide smooth brow.

'What happened?'

'It hasn't yet—this is the first test.'

She lifted her face and quivered nervously. *'Test?'* It had an ominous sound and brought back the terrible weeks of revision before her finals, then the elation of passing before she'd realised that exams were only the first step. Next came experience.

She'd been lucky and got a job offer after her first interview, a firm based in Edinburgh but with their heart and much of their work in the Highlands, domestic and commercial.

She'd joined a team of young and enthusiastic architects with innovative ideas for affordable but aesthetically pleasing homes in the Highlands.

She had seen her future as mapped out and then… Well, it just went to show that you should live in the moment. She had walked away from her dream job and did she regret it? She looked at the crumpled sleep suit in her hand and lifted her chin. Not for one second did she regret her choice.

'We are in love, remember.'

The soft words jolted her back to the moment with a thud. She dropped the sleep suit, gulped and tried to match his insouciant tone. 'I didn't think you'd care what the help thinks, and you've already told me that your grandfather doesn't believe in love... or is that you? You know, a person could be forgiven for thinking the brooding Latin lover doth protest too much.'

'I'm not your lover.' The blush she had held at bay couldn't withstand this provocation or the dark chocolate, velvety voice. 'As for the help, just don't smile at them the way you did those two.'

'Smile?' She shook her head, bemused by his comment. 'I don't...' Her voice faded as he took her arm and propelled her towards the open doors and onto the metal platform in the open air. 'My jacket!' she protested.

She didn't need it. The heat after the air-conditioned atmosphere of the flight hit her. She lifted her hand to shade her eyes against the sun. The men carrying the buggy were on the tarmac waiting; so were several other people. Oh, hell, she realised, a reception committee! All it lacked was a brass band and some sexy baton-twirlers.

This was more awful than any of the scenarios she had dreamt of.

'I'd assumed low profile,' he hissed through clenched teeth.

She felt his low chuckle, low *heartless* chuckle, and then his fingers tightened around her shoulder in warning, as though he had expected her to turn and run back into the plane. *Serve him right if I did,* she thought viciously.

'You might have warned me there would be...'

She had half turned and was tilting her head back when his hand moved from her shoulder to the back of her head, his long fingers curling into her hair and his thumb coming to rest on the angle of her jaw, making her forget what she was about to say.

He bent forward, the gleam of intent in his dark eyes telling her what was about to happen a split second before it did.

He was going to kiss her.

Then he did, and she stopped thinking.

His mouth was warm, his kiss managed to be slow and sensitive and yet possessive, a statement saying, 'She's mine,' to anyone watching.

Flora wasn't watching, she was *feeling*. It was as if her nerve endings had been exposed as she fell bonelessly into the kiss and him; resisting never even crossed her mind.

The hot stream of desire coursing like wine though her body was both terrifying and the most exciting thing that had ever happened to her.

His arms were like steel, holding her close, moulding her to his hard body, *very* hard. Knowing he was aroused—that he *wanted* her—only escalated her excitement, her *madness*.

And then it was over. The anticlimax had the physical impact of an icy plunge pool after a sauna.

She couldn't breathe, normality still felt a long way off and her brain was blank.

'You all right?' he asked as she swayed.

Bit too late to be concerned now, she thought as she glared her dislike up at him. Even in the open she was conscious of the electrical charge that still surrounded them. 'I don't like heights,' she retorted, swaying coltishly away from his steadying hand. The one that planted itself firmly in the small of her back was impossible to evade.

'All about first impressions, *cara*,' he whispered, running his lips up the curve of her neck. 'There are people here who will be reporting back to my grandfather.'

She was dimly aware in the distance of Jamie making his own first impressions as he kicked off— *loudly*!

'Jamie…'

He nodded and speared his free hand through his hair, wondering as he did at what point he had actually thought he was in control.

He was acting like some sort of hormonal teenager…or his father.

Short of hugging an iceberg, nothing could have exerted a more blood-cooling effect than the second possibility.

Flora listened as he responded to a question from someone standing inside the plane with what sounded like orders issued in his native tongue. She used the moments to gather her wits.

'Sorry about that,' he murmured as the person vanished.

'For kissing me?' she said, managing to sound cool, even slightly amused.

Was he sorry?

He ought to be. She was, it turned out, *exactly* the sort of woman he'd spent his life avoiding, the sort of woman of whom he could imagine men becoming reliant on the sound of her voice to start the day.

He wasn't one of those men. He had no emotional connection, it was just sex…or it had the potential to be.

'You'd be insulted if I said yes.'

Flora met his dark, hypnotic gaze and was lost. Great big holes appeared in the composure she had managed to gather around herself. Lowering her gaze was the only protective option left and that wasn't as easy as it should have been. By the time her eyes were safely fixed on her toes her skin was covered by a fine sheen of perspiration.

'I'm sure you enjoy performing to your adoring audience but, like I said, I'm not good with heights.'

'Come on. Watch your step.'

His hand stayed an inch clear of her elbow as she walked straight-backed down the steps, close enough to steady her should it be required and far enough away to avoid having another of her displays of pig-headed independence.

The meet-and-greet, the VIP fast route—actually everything that happened between walking down the metal stairs and getting into the middle one of the half-dozen cars that seemed to be reserved for their party—was a bit of a blur.

Was this what it felt like to be a celebrity? If so, Flora couldn't for the life of her work out why so many people wanted this dubious status.

She knew she'd been introduced to people she'd never seen before, and wouldn't know again, even though their names were drifting like flotsam through her head. She knew she'd smiled in what she hoped were appropriate moments.

Ivo spoke to the driver for a few moments before the screen separating them slid silently into place. He leaned back in his seat.

'That went well.'

Flora held out a toy, zooming it in to tickle the baby's tummy and nuzzle his cheek to distract him.

Ivo's proximity was bothering her too much. She really hoped this was a short journey. 'I think your idea of *well* and mine might be pretty far apart.'

'The kiss?' Head against the deeply padded leather rest, he turned his head.

'Yes, the kiss.' She had decided to treat it just like any other line that had been crossed. Making a big thing of it would *make* it big thing or, and that was what she was afraid of, make him realise that it *had* been a big thing for her—nothing short of a revelation.

He had tapped into a *passion* inside her. A *hunger* that she hadn't known existed. Even when she had imagined herself in love with Callum she had never considered herself a particularly sexual person. If she had been she might have been less appreciative of what she had idealistically assumed was his *consideration*. She'd realised later, of course, that he simply hadn't been into her that much.

'You want me to ask next time?'

'A little warning would have been appreciated, and maybe a breath mint.'

She was just feeling pleased with herself for keeping things light when he laughed; the deep vibrant sound sent illicit shivers down her spine. Then he touched her cheek and the contact seemed both natural and intimate. His eyes dropped to her lips. 'You tasted like strawberries.'

She fought the magnetic pull with a shocked little gasp to break the contact, before flopping back in her seat, breathing hard.

'So, what happens now?' she said, putting all the cool and practical at her command in her voice.

'Try catching up on some sleep.'

Her eyes went to the baby. 'I couldn't.'

'It might help some of those frown lines smooth out.'

'I suppose I might come across as a bit overprotective.' The concession came reluctantly and drew a short, hard laugh from her travelling companion.

'You think?'

She gave a little shrug. 'He's my responsibility and I was worried about him flying.' Not worried enough, she thought with a fresh rush of guilt.

The possibility that the tiny defect in his heart detected at Sami's twenty-week scan and confirmed at birth might make air travel an issue had not occurred to her until *after* Ivo had left that first morning.

Obviously she had contacted the family GP immediately, who, declaring himself unable to see a problem, had in turn checked with the paediatric cardiac consultant who had overall responsibility for Jamie's care.

His advice had been the same: there was no reason Jamie could not fly.

'Babies fly all the time.'

It was annoyance at his dismissal that made her toss back, 'Not all babies have a heart defect.'

The indolent pose he'd adopted vanished as his posture stiffened. 'A heart...' His chest lifted as he inhaled deeply before training his accusing stare on Flora. 'Why am I just learning of this?'

'Possibly because you never asked, or maybe because it's none of your business?' she charged back, angry at his display of *how very dare you?* hauteur.

The muscles in Ivo's brown throat rippled as he swallowed. He was still in the grip of shock, not just because of the information she had casually dropped into the conversation, but because of the overwhelming surge of protectiveness that had hit him without warning.

'Is he...is it bad?'

She shook her head. 'At Sami's twenty-week scan they discovered a small defect in the baby's heart.

Something they call a VSD, and the rest of us call a hole in the heart. Sometimes it's vanished by birth, but Jamie's hadn't. He was referred to a top cardiac paediatrician.'

It took a supreme effort but Ivo managed to stop himself asking any of the myriad questions that were hovering on the tip of his tongue. He knew that letting her speak would tell him what he wanted to know quicker, and she was being concise as she gave the information in a carefully neutral voice.

'It isn't that rare. In more severe cases they surgically intervene on infants. Jamie's isn't severe and there is every chance it will close spontaneously over the next few years. It's a wait-and-see policy at this stage and he has no symptoms.'

'So he is in no immediate danger.'

'No, the doctors are quite relaxed about it.'

'But you're not,' he said, leaning back into the leather and half closing his eyes. 'You have to relax. Babies pick up on that stuff.' He opened one eye and saw she was looking at him in astonishment. 'I've been doing a bit of research.'

The slightly embarrassed look on his face as he made the admission made her smile. It was weird—she had never known her emotions to be on such a roller coaster and it was all the unpredictable man's fault. One moment he was yelling at her and being totally unreasonable, the next he was being disarmingly sweet.

Her smile deepened as she realised she'd just thought of Ivo Greco and *sweet* in the same sentence.

'I did a lot of research when I first...' Her eyes skittered away from the understanding in his. 'When I became guardian. I knew nothing about babies. I never thought I'd be a parent. I never had a five-year plan or anything. I just sort of fell into things—right place, right time.'

She made it sound as though she had sleepwalked into a great job at an incredible firm of architects and graduated in the top three in her class quite accidentally. *God save me from British self-deprecation!*

Scottish self-deprecation, he could almost hear the pride and reproach in her voice as she put him right—as she undoubtedly would do, were he reckless enough to voice his complaint.

He opted for a middle ground.

'Modesty... I don't come across that very often.'

She scowled. He made her sound like some sort of old-fashioned freak. 'And definitely not when you look in the mirror.' Her eyes flew wide, her hand going to her lips in an attitude of comical dismay. 'Sorry. I didn't mean that as an insult.'

Amusement danced deep in his eyes as he studied her face and then faded like a snuffed-out candle as he found he was able to see all too clearly her checking and double checking on the sleeping baby, her glorious hair swinging loose around her narrow shoulders, tense from the burden that had fallen on them. He could almost see the individual lines of worry etched on her youthful, beautiful face as she

searched fearfully for signs and symptoms the doctors had told her to look out for.

Fighting his way free of the uncomfortably em-
pathic moment, he managed a forced smile.

'God help me when you *do* mean it, Flora Henderson.' His glance slid to the baby lying between
them just as his head lolled; this time he didn't jerk
himself awake as he had on the last half-dozen times.

'Why don't you take a nap while he's asleep?'

'I couldn't,' she said, meaning it.

Two minutes later he heard her breathing deepen.

CHAPTER EIGHT

'I SLEPT!' FLORA YELPED, coming to with a jerk after several moments of pleasant drifting.

One hand meshed in her tangled curls, she clenched the fingers of her right hand as her glance went straight to the sleeping baby. Seemingly satisfied, she relaxed, or at least went down from red to amber alert status...

When had she last relaxed?

Not his business, Ivo reminded himself. She was a consenting adult and if she chose to... Feeling his anger build, Ivo closed the laptop on his knee with a decisive snap. The illusion that he'd actually been working was false. The face of his sleeping travelling companion had been infinitely more appealing than emails or financial breakdowns.

He supposed there was an element of guilty pleasure, though mostly pleasure, in being able to stare at her unobserved. To study the curve of her cheek, the elegant arch of her brow and the pink bow of her mouth. He remembered how she tasted and wanted to taste her again. He imagined himself waking her up with a kiss.

Despite the Sleeping Beauty analogy, in his head there was nothing chaste or fairy-tale-like about the kiss, or her response! It involved warm pale limbs wrapping around him, sinking into…

'Are we nearly there?'

Wrenched free of the sensual, erotic images, he clamped his lips tight over a strangled laugh, and watched her *almost* press her nose to the window.

They'd been *there* for at least ten minutes. The fertile land dotted with fig groves and larger stretches of vineyards belonged to his family.

But he knew what she meant.

'We've just left the village.' At the foot of the craggy outcrop that the Castello was built on, much of the village still belonged to the Greco estate. 'Just wait a minute and you'll see it.'

She followed the direction of his pointing finger and turned her head.

Beside her Ivo said, 'About—now!'

He heard her breath catch; it was a common response to the first sight of his family home, but the awe on Flora's face made him think of a child seeing a Christmas tree.

Flora realised a moment too late that the open-mouthed look was not the height of sophistication, or for that matter a good look on anyone except, perhaps, her travelling companion, who would look incredible no matter what.

At least this was an example of life's unfairness that she could smile at, and she did smile as she shifted in her seat to face him.

'It looks like something out of a fairy tale. The towers...' Head shaking, she glanced back at the square stone towers at each of the four corner of the monumental building.

'They were there a couple of hundred years before the actual Castello. There's a view over the sea from up there, but it's not bad from here either.' He nodded past her and she turned again.

She'd been aware of the steep incline of the winding road but not the village, built on the edge of the water, it revealed or the glittering aquamarine sea scape it was set against.

Wow hardly seemed adequate—when he had spoken of Jamie's heritage she had never imagined anything like this. On this scale the historic grandeur was intimidating. 'So this is the Greco ancestral home.'

'There have been Grecos here for centuries. This place's fortunes followed ours, land sold, land bought back, disrepair and grandeur, but our family originally didn't build the place, an ancestor won it in a card game, or so the story goes. A tale probably invented for the tourists.'

'Have you always lived here?'

'We lived here as children, but these days I have an apartment in Florence. It's more convenient for when I'm in Italy, but I travel a great deal. I could give you a history but as an architect you'll probably know more about it than me.'

'I am an architect,' she agreed, wondering absently if this was the wrong tense, or maybe, considering the sick feeling in the pit of her stomach, to describe her as a *scared* architect would have been more appropriate. 'Not an art historian.' That said, she did recognise the massive double entrance that had come into view on top of an impressive flight of stone steps as a pretty incredible example of pure Renaissance.

The melding of styles over the years had given this place a unique look, in the same way the melding of genes over the years had given Ivo a unique look.

The thought drew her gaze towards the man whose genetic make-up had produced…well…perfection, and she found he was looking at her. He wasn't smiling and there was something in his eyes that made her heart beat faster.

She lifted her chin in response to the silent challenge glittering in his eyes. 'So what now?'

'Now we get you and Jamie settled. I'm assuming that Salvatore will want to see you both.'

An invitation where non-attendance was not an option.

Her spiky, thick lashes half lowered, her plump lower lip caught between her teeth, her soft mutter of, 'I can hardly wait,' was obviously not as under her breath as she intended because he responded drily.

'In order to avoid any misunderstandings, I should

mention that my grandfather is not likely to get *irony*, or, for that matter, humour.'

'Any more tips?'

'Don't overthink this, and don't look so guilty.'

She silently tacked on *and don't throw up* as she nodded to the uniformed figure holding the door open and slid out of the car.

A moment later Ivo joined her. He was carrying the car seat. She was actually grateful for the light pressure of the guiding hand in the small of her back as they approached the shallow flight of stone steps with the elaborate wrought-iron railings.

This was what Bruno had walked away from. Seeing it up close made her appreciate for the first time just how much he had turned his back on for the woman he loved, just what he had sacrificed.

She had thought that the home and business his parents had built was Jamie's inheritance, preserving it had been her focus, but now she was here she realised that *this* was Jamie's birthright too.

She glanced down at the baby sitting contentedly, his sun hat slightly askew on his dark curls, and experienced a moment of mind-clearing clarity.

Her chin lifted. Yes, she would fight to keep the business going, so that, unlike his father, Jamie would never have to choose. 'None of this actually matters. Jamie's true birthright is his parents' love.'

She hadn't been aware that she had voiced the realisation out loud until the pressure against her spine increased and Ivo's deep-voiced cynicism, etched in every syllable, floated down to her, making her wince.

'You put a high price on love.'

She was still blinking as she waited for her eyes to adjust to the more subdued light after the brilliant sunshine outside, when a man approached. *Neat* was the word that popped into her head when she saw him. Everything about him was precise, from his neatly trimmed beard to the parting in his slicked-back hair; she could have seen her reflection in his highly polished shoes.

'Ramon.'

'Sir.' He greeted Ivo with a deferential tip of his head.

'Flora, this is Ramon, my grandfather's major domo, who makes this place run like clockwork. Ramon, this is my fiancée, Ms Flora Henderson, and Jamie.'

'Hello.' The way he looked at the hand she had extended made Flora wonder if she had broken some sort of etiquette, but his smile was genial as he took it in a dry-handed grip.

'If you're here as an escort, Ramon, explain to my grandfather—'

'Jamie needs feeding.' Flora had been watching the baby push his chubby fist into his mouth. Experience told her they had about five minutes before the hungry wailing started.

'There, you see, my grandfather will have to wait.'

The older man cleared his throat. 'Of course.' He

nodded his head as three people appeared. They responded to instructions he delivered in his precise voice with lots of nods. 'Actually, sir, I was hoping… The doctor is here and your grandfather has given him permission to speak with you.'

Flora felt Ivo's splayed fingers tighten in the small of her back; her eyes went to his face. His features were still. Despite the lack of any discernible expression at all on his face, or maybe *because* of it, Flora sensed the emotions under the surface.

If everyone had a secret fear, she decided then that Ivo's was anyone who suspected he was human.

'You go,' she said, drawing the attention of the older man to herself. 'We'll be fine.' She stepped away from his supportive touch and curled her fingers around his on the handle of the baby carrier. 'I can manage,' she said and turned, while around them the rest of the luggage and baby paraphernalia was being carried up the stairs and along one of the wide galleries that ran around the upper floor perimeter, before vanishing.

'I can manage,' she repeated with another tug.

Ivo didn't release his grip but he did put the carrier down on the floor. 'Give us a moment, will you, Ramon?'

The other man moved away to a discreet distance.

Flora glanced over her shoulder towards him and, pitching her voice low, said softly, 'I'm sorry.'

He arched a brow. 'What for?'

'That your grandfather is…'

'What? Dying? Well, that's why you're here, isn't it? Smile, *cara*, this might be good news for you. I know you were too *polite* to ask how long but this does looks promising for you, so fingers crossed.'

It wasn't just the sneering intonation in his voice or the coldness in his eyes as they swept over her face, it was the fact that she hadn't seen it coming. She focused on stopping the tears she felt pressing at the backs of her eyes and told herself it was ridiculous to feel this level of hurt.

'Why are you being so hateful?'

He flinched inwardly at the unconscious dignity in her stance, but he ignored the guilt nudging his conscience and refused to even acknowledge the odd wrenching sensation in his chest as he looked down into the reproachful blue eyes that shimmered up at him, bright as jewels.

He gave a negligent shrug. 'What can I say? They tell me it's one of my talents.'

'Odd. I get the impression you're working hard at it.' The bewilderment in her face was genuine. 'Why are you pushing me away?'

Wishing the words unsaid, not even knowing where they had come from, Flora veiled her eyes as she pushed her way through a wave of cringing embarrassment by sheer force of will.

Pushing you away...! It was the sort of thing that people in a relationship said. She twisted the ring on her finger and reminded herself it was very much for show.

He flinched inwardly, then dealt with the direct hit the only way he could—he ignored it. 'Ramon.'

The other man hurried over.

Flora was aware of Ivo saying something to him but it wasn't until the dapper bearded figure reached for the baby carrier that Flora reacted. Possibly he was slow because he thought the request was beneath his pay grade, but Flora got there before him, tugging up the carrier in two hands and holding it against her front.

'I can manage.' Anger shimmered through her as she walked, stiff-backed, towards the staircase. A lot of things were uncertain but one thing she knew for sure: she was not going to waste her sympathy on Ivo Greco again, or imagine he was something he was not.

The doctor, actually two of them, stood outside his grandfather's bedroom. One he recognised as Salvatore's personal physician, the other was a stranger. If he'd had any doubts remaining, their professional expression, that blending of gravity and sympathy that all medics perfected, said it all.

Ivo took a deep breath and dragged a hand through his hair, banishing the lingering memory of the hurt in Flora's eyes that had plagued him as he'd walked down the corridors feeling like a total heel.

What was the British saying? *If the hat fits...*

Well, it did, he decided, removing his hand from his hair, not bothering to smooth down the spikes.

Flora's only sin in this instance was being in the firing line when he had realised this wasn't one of the old man's games, he really *was* dying, and rather than admit even to himself that he cared, his reflex had been to hit out.

Obviously at one level he had known that it was a possibility that for once in his life his grandfather was being forthright, and he should have been prepared, but deep down he had never actually believed that Salvatore, who had always seemed so indestructible to him, was dying.

The irony was he hadn't even known he was in denial until the moment he had heard the truth in Ramon's voice.

This wasn't just another of the old fox's schemes. It was for real.

Not quite the classic case of the boy crying wolf but a toxic, twisted version of it.

'He is waiting for you.'

Ivo never had responded well to authority, and this went double for the white-coated variety. He was not impressed by medical degrees. Men with more degrees than wall space had not stopped his damaged father killing himself or his mother dying. 'And yet you are out here.'

'We wanted to speak to you before you go inside. Actually, we wanted to speak to you much earlier, but we were constrained by your grandfather's wishes.'

That would be right, Salvatore would always have

the last word, even if that word was a dying word...
'Is it cancer?'

The men glanced at each other, then the one he
didn't recognise cleared his throat.

'I'm afraid not.'

Afraid? What the hell could be worse than cancer? Ivo wondered.

'Your grandfather has dementia.'

Ivo looked at him and laughed, not an amused
sound. 'That's the most ridiculous thing I've ever
heard. My grandfather is as sharp as a tack. He can
run rings around someone half his age, physically
and *mentally*.'

'Your grandfather can have long periods of lu-
cidity.'

*Meaning he doesn't know where he is the rest of
the time.* The grinding pain pressing into his temples
was no longer the beginning of a tension headache,
it was full blown. Ivo looked coldly at the man who
spoke before transferring his attention to the familiar face of the family doctor, who up to this point
had seemed reasonably reliable.

'I don't know where you dug this joker up from,
but I want a second opinion.'

The older man flushed and looked embarrassed
as he sent an apologetic grimace to his colleague.
'This is Professor Ranieri—'

Ivo arched a brow; the degree of reverence had
only increased his antagonism. 'Is that meant to
mean something to me?'

The younger man stepped forward. 'I'm a professor in neurodegenerative conditions and dementia, Mr Greco, and I *am* the second opinion.' He flashed his colleague a look. 'Or would I be correct in saying third is more accurate?' The older man nodded unhappily. 'I diagnosed your grandfather three months ago,' he finished quietly.

'He's suspected it for some time,' the older man added to back up his colleague. 'When he finally consulted me, well, the tests were all conclusive.'

Ivo's chest lifted, and he swallowed; his brain still refused to accept what he was being told. First Bruno and now Salvatore, a double whammy.

His family was vanishing.

He had not seen his brother for years, and he saw his grandfather as little as he could. Alone was the way he liked it, he reminded himself.

'I would have known.' He clung stubbornly to the belief because the option was believing what these men were saying.

'Not necessarily, Mr Greco. People with dementia will hide their symptoms—even those closest to them don't always notice. Some changes can be subtle.'

'No.' Ivo remained firm. 'We spoke last week, he was… He called me Bruno…' The recovered memory took on a new significance as he replayed highlights of the conversation in his head. Suddenly the clues were there, the minor errors evidence of his memory loss.

Ivo stood there breathing hard as his defences against the ugly truth disintegrated. He could no longer stop himself thinking of the tough old man with a razor-sharp brain losing part of himself and knowing it. It was the ultimate horror; fear clawed at his own belly just thinking about it.

Dio, Salvatore must have been desperate!

'Look, we appreciate this is a lot to take in.' The older man stepped forward to place a reassuring hand on Ivo's arm but was stopped by a look from those dark, hooded eyes. 'You'll need time to digest and there will be questions. We are accepting your hospitality for the night, so whenever you're ready?'

Ivo's jaw tightened. 'How about now?'

The older medic cleared his throat and adjusted the wire-framed spectacles perched on his nose. 'Actually, I believe you are expected inside.' He nodded towards the bedroom door. 'We are here at the behest of your father's lawyer.'

'Rafe is here?' Was he the last to know? Just how many people had known before he had?

'You grandfather wishes, I believe, to sign over power of attorney to you. That is why we are here, to confirm that his mind is… That he is able to make such a decision with sound mind and without any external pressure.'

Ivo struggled to hide the devastating impact of the wave of shock that rose up inside him like swirling filthy flood water. 'That is hardly urgent.' Right now, his priority was learning all there was to know about what his grandfather was facing.

Knowledge was power. There was always an alternative; this wasn't something that you meekly accepted.

It was the younger doctor who responded. 'Can I be frank with you?'

Ivo said nothing, he just looked.

'Right, well, tomorrow, Mr Greco,' he said gently, 'we might not be able to confirm that your grandfather has the mental capacity to make that decision. Time is running out, I'm afraid.'

CHAPTER NINE

I⊤ was ⊤wo hours before the lawyers, and Ramon who had acted as a witness, had the documents signed.

'Well, that's done.'

Ivo didn't say anything.

'So how does it feel, boy, to finally have the old man where you want him?' Salvatore mocked.

Suddenly Ivo was angry, too angry for a moment to respond. 'Is that what you think I am?'

'No, it isn't. I would be happier if you were. You're soft, Bruno, you always were. You allow emotions to get in the way of good sense.'

Ivo's anger dissolved as quickly as it had flashed. 'I'm Ivo, Grandfather.'

The old man looked away. 'What's in a name…? I didn't tell you because I didn't want anyone to know, for anyone to know that Salvatore Greco is a feeble-minded dribbling idiot who needs feeding.' His voice cracked.

Ivo turned away while his grandfather fought the tears that filled his eyes. He had never seen his grandfather cry. He was filled with a sense of help-lessness he had never felt before.

'You will not tell anyone. Swear to me, Ivo.'

Ivo turned back to face him. 'I swear.'

'Give me a little while longer before my enemies start celebrating. So, what is the child like?'

'Jamie is a...nice baby.'

'And you're marrying the girl.'

Ivo shook his head. 'No.'

'I thought as much. You're a devious devil. You get that from me. Is the baby like...his father?'

It wasn't seeing his grandfather struggle to remember his grandson's name, it was watching him try and disguise the fact that it felt like a body blow as a fresh stab of toxic guilt consumed him.

How could I not have seen this?

Ivo moved impulsively across the room to his grandfather's side. 'Grandfather—'

The old man held up his hands as though warding off danger, his lip curled in a snarl of distaste. 'No soft stuff and sentiment. I'm not totally ga-ga yet.'

His expression blank, Ivo drew back.

'That's better. I think I'll sleep. When does the boy arrive?'

'They are already here.'

'We will have dinner tomorrow, then.' He gave a little chuckle and threw his grandson a knowing look. 'Are you bedding her yet? Oh, my God, when you look down your nose at me you look just like my father. I was a major disappointment to him, you know, never good enough for him.' His voice trailed away. 'Too crude and vulgar.'

It was several minutes before Ivo realised he'd fallen asleep.

Ramon was waiting outside the door when he emerged. 'He's asleep,' he said.

'He tires easily.'

They exchanged a nod of understanding. Ivo took steps before the reality began to kick in; the entire empire was now his responsibility. The buck stopped with him.

The suite of rooms she had been allocated covered three floors, and had, as well as the master suite, two guest suites, a dining room, living room, kitchen, a kitchenette, a day nursery, a night nursery, lift access to the nannies' rooms and one to the ground floor.

When asked was it suitable she gave a cheery smile and said, 'Just like home.'

Nobody smiled at her joke but they did leave her in peace.

She focused on the immediate priorities. Bathing and feeding Jamie were top of the list, after which he'd immediately fallen asleep.

A hot shower was calling her. It was a relief to strip off her creased clothes and step into the shower after resisting the temptation of the massive antique copper bathtub. A long luxurious soak was for an occasion when Ivo was not likely to appear to bear her off to the awful interview with his grandfather.

When she walked back into the sitting room, wearing a soft robe from the bathroom, there were hot coffee and tea, tiny sandwiches and a selection of pastries on one of the tables.

She poured a black coffee, took a sip and, picking up one of the sandwiches, she went to the bedroom and walked over to one of the massive wardrobes. The scent coming from the lavender sachets that were hooked around the rail tickled her nostrils as she opened it. Someone had unpacked her clothes before she'd even reached the room and they looked pretty lost sitting there in the cavernous scented space.

Eating the rest of her sandwich, which was very good, she selected a dress similar in design to the creased one she had just taken off, though the neckline on this one was squarer and the fabric plain white with a discreet diamond pattern picked out in silver.

She fished out some fresh underwear and wriggled her way into it. It required a few contortions to reach the zip but once on she smoothed down the fabric and looked at herself in the mirror. She was playing a part. Did she look like the sort of woman a man like Ivo Greco proposed to?

The answer was quite obviously no, not when you considered the long-legged model types she'd seen hanging on him, quite literally in some instances, in the collection of photos available online for anyone interested enough to type in his name.

Now, if you were talking taking to bed...?

Fastening onto the unbidden thought came a flash-back to that kiss, as her gaze drifted to the big bed that dominated the room. She walked across and laid her hand on the smooth, pristine silk quilt.

Through half-closed eyes she visualised two figures lying there, limbs entwined. She shook her head to clear the erotic, illicit hallucination. A shiver ran through her body as she lifted a hand to her lips, running her finger along the outline, her eyes half closed.

What was happening to her?

Her breath came shallow and uneven as she fought against the pressure exerted by the knot of tangled emotions, among them a yearning she didn't want to acknowledge, all lodged behind her breastbone. It was as if that one kiss had released something inside her. Something she didn't seem to have any control over.

She wandered across to the dressing table and picked up a silver-backed brush. Removing the pins that had held up her hair in the shower, she began to brush it, focusing on the long soothing strokes and not the depressing realisation that that kiss had been the most mind-blazingly erotic experience of her life. Which had to make her one of the saddest twenty-five-year-olds in the world.

How many twenty-five-year-old *virgins* were left in the world, outside convents?

'You're an anachronism, Flora…and yet,' she told her mirror image, 'you look quite normal.' She waved the brush at the mirror. 'Freckled, and very ginger, but normal.'

She brushed until her hair prickled with static, a fiery nimbus around her face.

And she could still taste that kiss.

With a small, angry cry of self-disgust she threw the brush across the room. It landed bang in the middle of the big bed.

'This has to stop, Flora!' she told herself as she stalked across to retrieve it.

For some reason Flora found herself reluctant to put a crease in the pristine bed linen so, leaving one foot on the floor, she pushed her other knee through the folds of the dress and put it on the bed before she stretched out to reach the brush.

She was in this position when Ivo walked into the room.

What he had intended when he walked in, he'd never know because the moment he saw her there, the provocative image of her rear, the smooth curve of her bare thigh, the cloud of copper curls, he didn't fight it. It was a done deal.

It was with relief that he embraced it, actually ran full tilt at it. He wanted the mindless oblivion of sex, and that was all it was.

Wanting her.

She didn't see him. She saw his reflection in the mirror on the opposite wall and immediately lost her balance and pitched forward to land in a sprawled heap on the bed.

With a grunt of dismay she fought to pull the dress over her legs as she twisted over onto her back. Levering herself semi upright on her elbows, she looked across the room to where he stood. A combination of shock and excitement slithered through her, the way he was standing, the way he was breathing... She could feel the tension that was written in his face and in the tense muscles on his powerful body; the sense of danger that she'd always been conscious of in him was there but there was nothing potential about it, it was raw and real.

There was a moment of total silence as their eyes clashed, and connected, and then he was striding across the room, making her think of some sort of ancient Roman warrior.

He stood for a moment beside the bed, not saying a word. She looked at him, his image filtered through the skeins of hair that had drifted across her face, until he bent forward.

'I want to see you.'

The contact of his cool brown fingers on her hot skin as he brushed back the hair from her face was like a lightning strike. Every muscle in her body tensed, electrical shocks zigzagging through her.

'That's better,' he breathed, drinking in the delicate features turned up to him.

His voice seemed to be coming from a long way off, but it wasn't because she could feel his breath warm on her cheek as he pressed the heel of his hand against the centre of her chest and pushed her back-wards onto the bed.

It felt to Flora as though she were in slow motion. Everything had slowed, even her heart; each fresh beat of blood around her body felt like a drumbeat in her temples. She was more conscious of her own body than she ever had been, conscious of every-thing from the heat pooled between her legs to the fine downy hairs that stood on her arms.

Arm over arm, he dragged himself up the bed until his face was level with hers. With his body suspended over her she felt cut off from everything but this man, this man who released all these wild, raw, primal feelings inside her.

She squeezed her eyes shut but the feeling didn't go away.

'I don't feel like me,' she whispered.

He kissed her paper-thin, blue-veined eyelids.

'I didn't mean for this to happen,' he rasped.

If you didn't want anything to happen, why walk into the room, Ivo? No, this is exactly *what you wanted to happen, what you have wanted to hap-pen from the first moment you set eyes on her.*

'I want you.'

The throaty purr of his words sent a primitive thrill through her body.

Her blue eyes blinked open; the primal glow in his dark eyes sent her insides melting. Her breath came harder and she could feel his breath hot on her face.

Though they were not touching she could feel the quiver of tension in his lean body.

The leashed power, his sheer maleness, filled her with a longing she had no name for. Every cell of her body ached for him. She had never felt anything like this in her life.

When Callum had wanted to wait, he said because he *respected* her, she hadn't pushed it. She hadn't questioned it, because there had been a small part of her that had been relieved. She certainly hadn't felt as though she'd die if she didn't give herself to Callum. There had been no yearning, no desire to surrender totally to the hunger roaring inside her, to ease a deep, aching inner loneliness she hadn't even known was there until now.

She felt frightened and excited, the only reason she held back the burden of her embarrassing inexperience. Should she tell him? It was the possibility that he might reject her that tipped the balance. She couldn't risk that. She needed this to happen too much.

'I want you too,' she whispered, as, framing his face with her hands, she kept her eyes open as she kissed him.

For a moment he did nothing as her lips moved across his, then she felt a groan vibrate deep in his chest and he kissed her back with a frantic hunger, a driving desperation, that forced the air from her lungs and drew frantic little moans from her own throat.

He slid down beside her and, one hand hooked behind her head, he slid his free hand down over the curve of her body and pulled her hard against him to face him. He stopped kissing her long enough to tangle his fingers in her hair, to pull her face away so that he could look at her. She just stared at him raptly as he swept away the strands of hair from her face.

She touched his face, smoothing her fingers over the stubble on his cheek and jaw, fascinated by the strength, the beauty, of the angles and hollows.

Her throat ached as she looked at him. 'You're beautiful.'

His jaw quivered in reaction to her awed whisper. This might be just sex but he needed it—*her*—as much as he needed the oxygen he was dragging into his lungs. He had never experienced a passion as powerful and as all-consuming as the one that drove him now.

The whispered touch of his breath on the skin of her face before he kissed her was a delicious torture and she was so ready when he did cover her parted lips with his own that she whimpered with relief, the sound lost in his mouth.

Still kissing her, his mouth moving in a series of open-mouthed, warm kisses down the graceful column of her neck, he slid his hands under the dress she wore, easing the straps off her shoulders and exposing the angles of her collarbones and the upper slope of her breasts. Her skin had an alabaster glow, the clarity enhanced somehow by the sprinkling of freckles.

Desire roared inside him like an inferno as he held her passion-glazed eyes and then suddenly, expertly, he pulled them both to their feet so that he could reach around her to ease the zip of her dress undone. He watched hungrily as the garment slid to the floor, leaving her standing in just her underwear. She shivered as the cool air hit her hot skin… and then shivered again when his hooded glance dropped to her chest. Her nerve endings reacted to the sensuous sweep of his hooded eyes as it would a touch.

'You're beautiful.' He reached round behind her, unclasping her strapless bra, and watched appreciatively as her breasts were fully exposed to him.

He tilted her back towards the bed and laid her down. His hands resting either side of her shoulders, his body was suspended above her, not touching… She wanted to touch him.

Did she say so? She had no idea, but he suddenly kissed her hard and levered himself off her and stood by the bed.

Her dismay switched to relief as he began to tear off his clothes.

Lying there, her only covering a tiny pair of pants, her breasts lifting and falling in time with her short, shallow inhalations, she watched him kick himself free of trousers and fight his way out of his shirt. The intoxicating wildness pumping through her bloodstream made her feel light-headed, reckless, unlike herself. She was literally paralysed with lust and longing. It infiltrated every cell of her body, every inch of her skin.

She ached for him in a way she hadn't known existed.

He paused for a moment by the bed, giving her greedy eyes the opportunity to gloat over his stream-lined perfect body, every muscle beautifully defined under skin that glowed gold.

One knee on the bed, he leaned over and ran his fingers under the waistband of her knickers, sliding them slowly down over her smooth thighs.

The first skin-to-skin contact made her gasp then sigh as he kissed her, his tongue slipping deep between her parted lips.

She grabbed his head to deepen the pressure of her tongue meeting his.

The soft keening moan of protests when his head lifted dissolved into a deep moan as he cupped one breast in his big hand, and, drawing a thumb up to the aroused rosy peak, he covered it with his mouth. By the time he moved to apply similar treatment to the other breast, she was writhing. The only thing stopping her floating away was his hand on her hip.

'Look at me, *cara*,' he slurred thickly.

His searing stare held her blue eyes tight as his hand slid between her legs.

'You feel ready for me,' he said, stroking her.

'I feel on fire,' she rasped. 'This is too…too…

much!' Her eyelashes fluttered against her cheek as he eased a finger into her.

'So tight,' he murmured against her ear. 'Incredible.'

She moved restlessly, pressing against his hand, not realising what else he was doing until he curled her fingers around him.

A choking sound of shock vibrated in her throat.

'That's how much I want… I need you. I want to be inside you, *cara*.' He could not remember wanting a woman this much in his life. It felt like a fever roaring in his blood, driving him to the act of possession. Teeth clenched, he fought the need, wanting her to need this as much as he did. His skin was slicked with sweat by the effort of staying in control.

No woman had ever tested his control this much.

The dark, driven need in his face increased her excitement. Her skin was on fire…she was burning up with need from the inside out. 'I need you too,' she gasped faintly.

As he rolled her beneath him she arched up into him. The touch of his body against the curls at the apex of her legs brought her eyes wide open and on a collision course with his hot, hungry stare.

'Please,' she said simply.

She felt the deep, animal groan building in the vault of his chest and it emerged at the same moment he slid into her.

She jerked, gasped and wrapped her legs around him. Eyes tight, focused on each advance and retreat, each thrust taking her deeper into herself. She focused on the places he was touching that had never been touched, the muscles that clenched by instinct, building the pressure, the pleasure, the nerves that were singing, the tension that was building and building.

She forgot where she ended and he began and it felt as if she couldn't bear any more, and then she saw explosions behind her closed eyelids, bursts of light as the heat and pleasure rocked through her body, as the pleasure centre in her brain went into overload.

The floating back to earth was gentle, as was his kiss before he rolled off her. They lay there, side by side on their backs, fingertips touching as their sweat-slick bodies cooled.

'So.' He propped himself on one elbow and looked down at her deliciously flushed face, remembering the look of concentration on her face as the heat had built inside her. His body stirred lazily, and then not so lazily as his glance slid a little lower. The sheet ended just below her coral-tipped, perfect breasts; they quivered as she covered her face with both hands.

The *lazy* element vanished at the quivering. His hunger for her had flared into full, hot life.

'Look at me, Flora.'

She dropped her hands and did. It would always be a pleasure to look at him, but right now it was a struggle to meet his gaze.

'I suppose you're talking about the virgin stuff.'

'You suppose right...' He adjusted a pillow and put it behind his head. 'I was under the impression that you'd had a love affair, were engaged.' He'd certainly not imagined there had been only one man in her life, so the discovery that he was her first lover had been one of the biggest shocks of his life.

He looked down and found she was looking up at him quizzically. 'Do you mind?'

Mind?

On one level it was possibly the most erotic thing in the world to know you were a woman's first lover...maybe modern man was a myth?

He swallowed. It fascinated him that this seemed a bigger thing for him than her. 'A heads-up might have been an idea. It's not usual to be a virgin at your age unless you have just come out of a nunnery.'

'Or you had a Callum in your life.' She sighed, with an eye roll and a supple feline stretch that sent a fresh slug of lust through his sated body.

She made him greedy.

'Callum?'

He'd never liked that name.

'All the girls at my school had a crush on Callum. He was seven years ahead of me, so he left as I arrived at high school. But his dad was our postman and his mum worked in a chemist in Portree. You'll ken that Skye isn't such a big place.'

'I ken.'

'Are you mocking me?'

He held up his hands in mock horror and promised solemnly, 'I wouldn't dare.' It flickered through his head that sleeping with a virgin wasn't the only *first* for him today; he'd never enjoyed, and, yes, he *was* enjoying, a post-coital conversation quite like this before.

Actually, his experience of post-coital conversations was pretty limited. His lifestyle was not about lingering, more perpetual motion. Lingering for him generally involved checking his emails.

'Anyway, I had a massive crush on him.'

At this artless confidence Ivo felt some of the pleasure of the moment slip away.

'We all did. I was in my second year at uni when I bumped into him, and, well, a month later we were engaged.' She closed her eyes. 'I know it sounds crazy. And it was. It turns out we expected very different things from marriage.' Callum wanted kids and she couldn't give him them.

Ivo caught her hand and nudged the diamond on her finger with his own. 'We were engaged in one day.'

She pulled her hand away and bent so that he couldn't see her face as she twisted the diamond around on her finger. 'That's not the same. *This*—' her clear blue gaze lifted to him '—is a...not a real... not real at all,' she finished awkwardly.

What had just happened felt *very* real. It felt very *right*.

'So, we just had imaginary sex.'

She flashed him a look. 'You know what I mean.'

He knew more than she realised. Reading between the lines it was pretty obvious that she'd told this Callum guy she couldn't have kids and he'd said, thanks but, no, thanks!

The bastard, he thought viciously.

'Well anyhow he…' She hesitated, after the Callum fiasco she had told herself that in the future she would tell any potential partner upfront that she couldn't have children. She hadn't quite worked out the timing yet, should it be on the first date, third, before you'd got to like him?

But she reminded herself before self-pity kicked in that timing was not an issue here. Ivo wasn't a potential partner, he was her lover. Her marvellous, incredible lover, but this was just sex, at least for him.

She felt a sudden spurt of panic and she didn't want to go where that acknowledgement was leading.

'Dumped me.'

Ivo's jaw began to ache as he watched her produce a smile that invited him to share the joke. Ivo did not feel in a joking mood, he recognised there was no reason for her to confide in him, he was the last person in the world to advocate trust, which begged the question, why? Though for a while there he had been holding his breath willing her to.

'I suppose it turned me off the whole dating thing, and since then I've been too busy to do anything about it.'

'So why didn't your mad, passionate love affair involve sex?'

'Other than the obvious truth I know now, that he just wasn't that into me? I think Callum is one of those men who think there are two sorts of women: the ones you sleep with and the ones you marry and then cheat on.'

'Charming guy.'

'I have terrible taste in men,' she agreed, snuggling into his side. No longer sweat-slicked, his cooled skin had a satiny texture that fascinated her, as did the movement of fine muscles just below the silky surface. Everything about him fascinated her to a point that she would previously have called obsession.

'Thank you.'

'Oh, it's fine. I'm not looking for a keeper and that was… Actually, you were totally marvellous.' It wasn't as if she was telling him something he didn't already know.

'You just insulted me and buffed my ego in one sentence. That takes skill.'

'So do you.'

At the last moment she lost her nerve and lowered her gaze.

'I am quite happy to pass my skills on.'

Her head lifted. 'Yes, please.'

CHAPTER TEN

IVO FOLLOWED RAMON out of the room. Flora had already vanished into the bedroom to change, ignoring his assurance that the jeans and silk shirt she was wearing were fine for breakfast with his grandfather.

'So, breakfast? I was under the impression that we were coming to dinner.'

Ramon tipped his head in acknowledgement. 'Yes, your grandfather informed me of this last night and asked me to arrange matters, but—'

'But…?' Ivo prompted.

'This morning he… He had forgotten.'

'Does this happen often?'

'More than it did,' said the other man, unhappily.

'What else have you noticed?' Ivo gave a brooding frown. He would respect his grandfather's wishes but it was inevitable that people would start noticing.

'Well, some mood swings—he can be quite…irritable.'

'Not exactly unusual.'

'Indeed, but, well, he can get ideas. Take against people.'

'Such as?'

'This is different. It is…'

'Go on, say it.'

'I am not a medical man, but it's more like *paranoia*. There was a new staff member, young, really very promising, and your grandfather decided that he had stolen his watch. He became quite abusive and accused the lad of being part of a conspiracy. The watch was in his dressing room where he always keeps it.'

'You smoothed things over?'

Ramon nodded.

Ivo, his expression sombre, heaved a sigh. 'I'm grateful and I'm sorry. This is not your job. I'll speak to the doctors, ask about extra staff. More qualified staff.'

A look of visible relief passed across the other man's face. 'That seems like an excellent idea, sir— and, sir, I suggested breakfast because that's a good time for him usually."

Madre di Dio, things really were that bad, and they would only get worse.

His grandfather would suffer, but for how long the doctors had been frustratingly vague.

And he could do nothing.

Except keep his grandfather's secret.

Ramon cleared his throat delicately and nodded past Ivo, looking at the half-closed door. 'May I ask, does Ms Henderson…?'

'No, not yet.'

Would it be the right thing to do in this situation?

The question in his head wasn't what was the right thing to do. Or even was there a right thing…he left moral philosophy for the better qualified.

If she knew the truth, what would her reaction be?

One thing was for certain: it wouldn't be a selfish one. If he'd learnt anything about the woman who had shown more passion in his bed than any other lover he'd had, it was that she was a born giver. She had to have arrived in the world with a note saying 'use me' in her chubby little hand.

And he had and furthermore he had enjoyed it. She was right, she did have terrible taste in men but *he* wasn't about to kick her out of his bed.

What a saint, admired the ironic voice in his head.

All right, he was no saint, but he was not this Callum guy who, he suspected, she might still have feelings for. The idea might have bothered a jealous man; luckily Ivo was a stranger to that emotion.

'I see.'

Ivo tipped his head in acknowledgement and began to step back inside the room, but it appeared that the relief of being relieved of some of the burden he'd been shouldering had made the normally taciturn Ramon uncharacteristically talkative and emotional.

'That must be hard for you.'

It didn't seem to require an answer so Ivo said nothing.

'Keeping secrets from the person you love, not

being able to share the burden, your grief. I had someone once, but no longer… I envy you.' Ramon gave another precise little nod, slightly embarrassed-looking this time, and walked away.

Ivo watched him go. If he'd felt the need to reach out to Flora…a woman, *any* woman, he would have crushed it instantly. He had no desire to be part of a relationship where two people blurred into one. The mere idea was anathema to him. He realised this romantic ideal of a joining of souls was what many dreamt of, but to him it represented a loss of control, of sanity, of the essence of his individuality.

The only merging he wanted was of bodies.

When he walked back inside his face was carefully blank, denying there was any struggle going on inside him.

Ivo was tense about the breakfast; the conversation with Ramon had made him realise that his grandfather was a lot more unpredictable than he'd realised.

It sounded as though his behaviour was such that, had he not been who he was, rich, powerful and pretty much a law unto himself, had he not surrounded himself, with a few exceptions, with people who would have agreed if he'd called day night, people might already be asking questions.

Or if you, his only family, had been around a bit more.

Ivo took the hit of guilt, pretty sure he deserved it. He need not have worried; the breakfast couldn't have gone better. Nobody meeting Salvatore for the first time would have known there was anything wrong. If he misspoke a few times…well, people did.

He was charming, funny and full of praise for Flora and the job she was doing. And he was emotional when he got to hold his great-grandson, who he decided looked exactly like his father, at which point he became tearful.

His tears evoked a sympathetic response in Flora, who didn't know that Salvatore never usually cried.

Ivo, worried about the mood shift, found himself moving protectively to Flora's side as she lifted the baby off his grandfather's lap, whereupon Jamie began to cry.

Ivo could have kissed the baby for his excellent timing. Salvatore did and then began to weep again.

'He's lovely,' Flora said, sending up a reproachful look to the man walking beside her. 'I can't believe how nervous I was, and he looks quite well…?' She hesitated a little before adding huskily, 'He's not in pain, is he?'

Ivo shook his head. Then, seeing the look of concern on her face as she pressed her fingers to the back of the baby's neck, he asked sharply, 'What's wrong?'

'Does he look flushed to you?'

Ivo didn't say anything. Jamie clearly did to her.

She touched his neck again. 'He feels hot to me,' she fretted.

Ivo could hear the panic in her voice. 'He looks fine to me.'

She shrugged off the hand he'd placed on her shoulder and shook her head, missing his reaction to the rejection.

'You're worried?'

She shrugged her slender shoulders and lifted her troubled eyes to the figure standing with his back to one of the windows against the distant background of the blue sea.

He looked so big, so solid and so calm that she felt a little of her panic subside.

'Sorry, you must think I'm crazy.' She loosed a self-mocking laugh. 'I used to wonder how I'd cope if Jamie was ill and I was alone, now I know I'd panic.'

'For starters, we don't know he's ill and you're not alone...or panicking...' He shook his head. 'Borderline at best.'

Not alone. She didn't make the mistake of reading anything into that, although the wistful feeling his words had shaken loose remained.

'It's just his heart. I'm sure it's nothing to do with that.'

'You'll feel a lot surer after the doctors have seen him. Leave it to me.'

Despite the fact she had told herself that morning that one thing she was not going to do was become too reliant on Ivo, she found herself sighing with relief.

'Thank you.'

This time she turned her cheek into the hand that an instinct he couldn't control had made him place on her shoulder, despite the earlier rejection. The re-action to feeling her soft cheek against his skin was just as strong and unexpected a reaction as her ear-lier rejection had been.

He let his hand fall away and stepped back.

'I'll organise it, then. You have the name of your GP and Jamie's consultant?'

She nodded and gave them. 'I don't have any paper.'

'Don't worry, I'll remember them.'

When the doctor arrived, a mere thirty minutes later to Flora's relief, she was dreading having to explain, especially if there was a language problem.

There wasn't and he seemed to have a full grasp of Jamie's medical history.

A very short time later, and after a thorough ex-amination of the by now cranky baby, he confirmed that the baby did have a mild fever and diagnosed a virus…basically a cold.

'And his heart?'

'No problem there that I can detect. When is his next appointment?'

'Six months' time.'

'Well, you are in good hands and this young man has a fine set of lungs. I knew Bruno, a good man, tragic, so tragic.'

Flora, her throat thick with emotion and unshed tears, nodded.

'So the analgesic syrup four-to-six hourly, keep

him cool and lots of fluids, any problems, you know where I am.' He glanced towards the sitting room where Ivo, who had not accompanied him into the nursery, was waiting. 'Or at least Ivo does. Those of us who know him were pleased to hear about his engagement and I am even more pleased now I have met you.' His charring smirk faded as he added, 'Ivo has few friends but those who are would die for him. He pretends he doesn't care but he—well, I don't have to tell you this, do I? Have you known him long?'

Blinking at this extraordinary endorsement and realising that nothing he'd said had surprised her, Flora shook her head. She already knew that Ivo's mask of toughness, and coldness, hid deep feelings, but she also knew that he'd never share those feelings, or at least not with her. 'No.'

'Well, it doesn't take long, does it, when you meet the right one?'

'No, it doesn't.' Flora said the words quickly because she didn't want to think about them too hard.

Quickly, but not quick enough to stop the flood, the relentless stream of images that began to flicker across her retina.

She blinked, her jaw tight as she struggled to halt the slide show. It felt as if a tug of war were going on in her head. She was pulling one way and...*truth* was pulling the other.

She couldn't have fallen in love; she hadn't put Ivo on a pedestal; she wasn't blind to his faults. She didn't even like him a lot of the time. She was just getting carried away by the great sex.

'So, everything good?'

She started guiltily and swung around, the rope of plait that hung down her back whipping around a moment after she did, landing with a thump over one shoulder.

She saluted him with the bottle of baby medicine in her hand. 'Yes.' Jamie, lying in the crib, chose that moment to give a cranky cry. 'He has a cold.'

'Let me.'

She watched as he bent over the crib, lifting the sobbing baby with the sort of care normally reserved for an unexploded bomb, his expression fierce concentration as he arranged the baby against one broad shoulder and began to pat his back gently. The sight of Ivo cradling his tiny nephew made her smile despite the hand squeezing her heart.

One day he would have babies of his own; crazily the thought made her want to cry.

He glanced across, a look of self-conscious enquiry drifting over his face when he saw Flora standing there staring. 'Am I doing it wrong or something?'

Flora swallowed the lump in her throat. How crazy to get choked up, but the sight of this big tough man being so gentle with the baby scored a direct hit on her tender heart.

'No, you're doing it perfectly,' she said, grabbing the first thing to hand, which was a baby blanket. She began to fold it as though her life depended on perfectly aligned creases. 'You know, you're welcome in Skye any time. You should be part of Jamie's life.'

Even before she heard his steely, 'I intend to be,' Flora sensed the change in the atmosphere. Maybe Jamie did too because he gave another whimper as Ivo laid him carefully down in the crib.

He watched Flora drag a chair over to the crib. They'd found mind-numbing passion together, and it was the thought of losing that and nothing else that had made him react to the idea of her vanishing back to Skye. That, after all, was the plan. Flora was to vanish out of his life, out of Jamie's life.

Was he being fair to Jamie?

A child needed a female influence and not just one supplied by nannies. There was no doubt that Flora was utterly devoted to the baby. He shook his head; in some ways his grandfather's plan was simpler.

Simple because Salvatore is losing his mind. The real question is: are you, Ivo?

He took a deep breath. He really needed to show her what an excellent life Jamie could have without her. It shouldn't be that hard. He'd show her the glossy brochure of the really excellent school he'd picked out for Jamie, Ivo decided.

What's the betting she disapproves of boarding schools?

'He might take a while to settle.'

'You planning on spending the night there?' Ivo pointed to the lift doors at the end of the room, the ones that led to nannies on tap. 'Or are you going to take some help?'

She pushed away a frivolous mental image of nannies lining up to slide down a pole like firemen, white frilly aprons fluttering, and started to shake her head.

'Look, I know you have strong feelings on the subject.' As she did on everything. 'But there is help there ready and waiting if you change your mind. I know I'm probably wasting my breath, but you have nothing to prove. Everyone can see you put the baby above everything else.' How many men would see that as a problem? An image of some future lover being jealous of Jamie drew his dark brows together in a frown.

'But you can accept help. You don't have to be a wonder woman or too tired and worn down to do fun things with the baby.'

Was he telling her that she looked worn down or she wasn't fun, or both?

'Or I could help?' he heard himself say.

The offer made her smile. 'Do you know one end of a nappy from the other?' she asked, ignoring the fact that a few weeks back she hadn't either. It was quite nice to feel superior for once. 'Stick to what you're good at.'

'I'm good in bed, or so someone told me not so long ago.'

The blush on the outside was visible but it was the heat deep down inside that was more of a problem for Flora, who brought her lashes down in a protective shield, but not before Ivo had seen the aching longing reflected in the blue depths.

Inhaling through his flared nostrils, he fought to leash his libido. In another woman he might have imagined the look of silent yearning was a calculated seduction technique, but Flora didn't have a clue what she was doing, or what power she was wielding.

It made her a very dangerous woman.

'Do you really think this is an appropriate moment for that sort of…?'

The striking contrast between the silent sensual message of her eyes and the prim, prissy delivery drew a laugh from his throat. 'Thing?' he suggested. His shoulders lifted in an expressive shrug. 'You could be right.'

She decided one concession deserved another. 'Maybe another pair of hands would be useful. Ones who know what they're doing, that is.'

The girl who delivered her meal gave a shy smile as she placed the tray down on the table on the balcony.

'Nanny Emily says you need the calories, that you're too stick thin. Me, I think you have a lovely figure,' she added daringly, straying from the party line.

'Thank you.'

Flora lifted the silver dome. Whatever was in the herby tomato sauce smelt good. She looked at the label on the wine bottle beside the single glass; presumably Nanny Emily saw nothing wrong in being drunk in charge of a baby.

And it would have taken a brave person to argue with the woman who radiated a reassuring sense of calm and spoke fluent Italian with a Yorkshire accent, which was fascinating to listen to.

She had made the day a lot easier but Flora had insisted that she take the night shift, rejecting the offer of a night nanny.

Finding it weird and a little worrying how quickly she had accepted the existence of night nannies and night nurseries, she had not objected when Nanny Emily had had a bed made up for her on the day-bed in the nursery.

She ate her lonely supper, picking at the food and allowing herself one glass of the really excellent red, which might have been a mistake because she found her thoughts veering towards self-pity. It wasn't as though she hadn't got plenty of practice eating alone, and Nanny Emily had offered to stay and keep her company.

Only it wasn't Nanny Emily she was imagining sitting opposite her in the empty chair.

She shook her head, tossed back the dregs of the wine and wandered back to the bedroom. The whole place was wired for sound; she'd have heard Jamie if he'd cried, but she went to check on him anyway. He was fast asleep, his poor little nose bright red, but when she touched the back of his neck he seemed cooler.

She adjusted the speed on the cooling fan and went over to the neatly made up bed. She didn't bother undressing, even though someone had brought night clothes from her room. Instead she lay on top of the covers intending to just rest her eyes.

Apparently, his grandfather hadn't been sleeping. His valet, a sombre-faced little man who'd been with his grandfather for ever, had to know something was wrong and yet when he asked him what he was doing standing in the corridor at one o'clock in the morning, the man had replied with no expression at all that his master had locked him out, as though it was the most normal thing in the world—it probably was for him.

'I'm just waiting to see if—'

Ivo shook his head. 'You go to bed and I'll check if he wants anything.'

'I need to put his clothes out for tomorrow.'

'Go to bed.'

The door was locked, but Ivo found his way in via a side door that led directly to the study. The study was empty but what seemed significant to Ivo was the debris of paper spread across the desk. He'd never seen that desk without neat piles and sharpened pencils in neat rows.

The TV was blaring in the drawing room but it too was empty. He eventually found his grandfather sitting on a stool in the bedroom, staring out into middle distance.

'Not sleeping.'

Salvatore didn't seem to find it strange to see his grandson standing there. 'Can't seem to these days. I think,' he added in a conspiratorial tone, 'they put something in the water. I'm seeing the baby tomorrow. Have they arrived?'

'Yes, Grandfather, they have. The baby has a cold.'

'Don't call the doctors, they're damned quacks.'

Ivo's knuckles turned white as he clasped them in front of himself. This was the man who had always seemed like a giant to him growing up, feared, but respected. To see him reduced to this was more than heartbreaking; it was tragic, it was cruel.

There were still people who clearly respected him, perhaps even loved him—what else but love would make someone carry on serving him with unquestioning loyalty?

The man they were loyal to was vanishing.

'How about you go to bed?'

It was an hour and a half later before Ivo finally left; his grandfather was asleep and Ivo knew he couldn't offload the responsibility that was his. He needed advice from people who knew about this evil disease.

He needed... He walked past the corridor that led directly to his own suite.

The lights in the nursery were turned down low when he entered. He walked over to the cot where the baby lay and then past it to the day-bed where Flora, fully clothed, lay sleeping.

He stood there for a while looking down at her, conscious of the ache located in his chest as he studied her sleeping face, the delicate contours and fine bones. Her beauty was compelling, the misleading fragility rousing protective instincts even though he knew she was a lot tougher than she looked.

Something inside him responded to her beauty the way it had from the first moment he'd seen her. He'd been as powerless to control it then as he was now, as he felt the swell of a nameless emotion build in his chest.

A shudder passed through him.

What the hell are you doing here, Ivo?

He was in no mood to analyse; emotionally drained dry by the encounter with his grandfather, he was operating on autopilot. Instinct had brought him here and the same instincts kicked in now.

The day-bed was narrow but he slipped into the narrow space beside the wall, slid a hand under her waist and pulled her back into him. Her soft body adjusted into his angles as she turned her head, her eyes opened and she saw him.

'Ivo!' Her voice, thick with sleep, was barely more than a husky whisper.

He put a finger to her lips and whispered, *'Hush.'*

The tension drained from her body as she closed her eyes, pushed her head against his shoulder, gave a sleepy murmur and went back to sleep.

Lying there with the scent of her hair in his nostrils, her body curved into his, he felt a strange sense of something close to peace drift over him.

He had no idea what had driven him here, or maybe pulled him here. The idea of losing himself in a woman's body made sense, but this physical but non-sexual embrace was outside his experience. Before he could sort it out in his head he fell asleep to the sound of Flora's soft, even breathing.

He slept deeply, before fighting his way through layers of sleep and into painful wakefulness; the arm she lay on was numb and heavy and there was a sour taste in his mouth.

He slid his arm from under Flora and slipped off the narrow bed. He looked down and felt the emotions inside him swell and begin to seep out, his jaw clenched as he tried to tap into his ability to turn his feelings on and off.

Nothing happened.

Instead he was forced to reel them in through sheer-minded willpower. The effort brought a sheen of sweat to his face but at least he had control again.

He'd been on the point of falling into the inevitability trap; 'the heart wants what the heart wants' nonsense was pretty much a version of crossing your fingers when you lied through your teeth.

A lie was still a lie, and a bad decision was still a bad decision. It all stemmed from the mawkish need for people to romanticise what was a basic primal drive.

He wanted, he *needed* sex. They had chemistry—

strong chemistry. There was nothing wrong in wanting sex; the *wrong* came when you imagined it was
going to last a lifetime.

A man had a choice, he reminded himself. He
didn't *have* to fall in love. There was strength in
being alone, not relying on anyone else to make you
happy. He was already complete. Love was a trap
that he was not about to fall into.

He'd always been able to separate his emotions
from basic needs, like sex, before. Then it came to
him, so obvious that he didn't understand why he'd
not seen it earlier!

The only reason this felt different was the fact
there was another factor between them. His eyes
went to the cot. He felt a connection because there
was a connection, not a deep, meaningful, heavenly
choir-singing one, but a physical one. Jamie!

He let out a long hissing sigh of relief.

He didn't look back because he didn't want to. He
wasn't trying to prove anything to himself.

The cold morning light was seeping into the room
through a window where the blind had not been
drawn. She could hear the sound of the dawn cho-
rus outside. She yawned and stretched, easing the
kinks out of her spine.

Her eyes suddenly snapped open.

Had she dreamt it?

The memories drifted through her head like

smoke, the impression of being held, of feeling warm and safe.

'Good morning, my dear, did you sleep? How was he?'

'Nanny...' Flora pulled herself up into a sitting position and swung her legs over the side of the narrow metal bed. 'He slept through, and so,' she admitted, removing a sharp object that had been sticking into her arm from her top, 'did I.' She rubbed her arm, was about to toss the object into the waste-paper basket when a glitter caught her eye.

She opened her palm.

It hadn't been a dream.

It hadn't been a dream—the beaten copper cuff-link she had first noticed gleam against the pristine cuff of Ivo's shirt lay in her hand.

She slid it into the pocket of her jeans, got to her feet and went over to the cot. Her thoughts were racing. When had Ivo come and how long had he stayed?

'You go and have a shower, dear, and take your breakfast. I'll feed him for you and wait for the doctor.'

CHAPTER ELEVEN

Ivo HAD STOPPED by his grandfather's office on his way to the nursery. He'd made some tentative enquiries today. If yesterday had taught him anything it was that he was going to have to bring some people in on the secret.

And therein lay the problem: it *was* a secret.

Her evening meal arrived at the same time as the previous evening. She had just lifted the dome when the door opened. Ivo took the cover from her hand and put it back down over the food.

'That looks terrible.'

She pulled in a taut breath before she lifted her gaze to the man who stood there looking out-of-this-world attractive.

The sight of him in a beautifully cut pale grey business suit, the formality softened by the open collar of his white shirt, was a signal for her hormones to go wild.

She swallowed, but found there was no moisture

in her mouth. Instead she ran her tongue nervously over her dry lips. 'It looks delicious.'

He picked up the wine bottle and looked at the label. 'I think we can do better than this.'

'I'm not drinking.' She really didn't need her inhibitions loosening; she needed them shoring up. 'Help yourself.'

'I'm driving.'

'Don't let me keep you,' she said, feeling pretty stupid for assuming he was here to keep her company.

He pulled out a chair and straddled it. 'We're eating out.'

She shook her head. 'I can't.'

'Why?'

'Isn't that obvious?' she flared back.

'Humour me.'

'Jamie…'

'They tell me his temperature is down and he's looking much better.' He arched an interrogative sable brow. 'Is that not right?'

'He needs a familiar face…he…' The impact of his male aura was so strong that she was only just seeing the tension in his face evident in the fine muscles around his jaw and the lines etched around his sensual, sculpted mouth.

'He what?' he prompted.

'I wouldn't feel comfortable leaving him at the moment.'

'Has it occurred to you that poor Jamie might need a break from you?'

She fought the urge to respond to his smile.

'Look, you've been here a few days now and you've seen nothing but the inside of the nursery. If there's a problem we'll only be five minutes away. Come on, you're going stir crazy, admit it.'

'Jamie still looks very pale.'

'So do you.'

The hungry intensity of his scrutiny made her stomach flip. She lifted a self-conscious hand to her face. If he thought this was pale he should have seen her before she'd put the blusher on, but then he had— he'd seen her in the night.

'But—'

He surged to his feet, all restless energy and testosterone making her feel dizzy. He looked, she decided, like a man with a lot on his mind.

'No buts, it's all arranged. Nanny Emily will take first shift and Olivia will sleep in the nursery. You need a night off.'

'But I'm not dressed.' And she had the start of a tension headache—lack of sleep, probably.

Lack of *something*!

Sadly, she was dressed.

He watched as she smoothed down the fabric of the slip dress over her thighs with a telling nervy, jerky motion, while calculating which would be the quickest way to remove it. Slide the straps over her shoulders and tug, or over her head in one smooth motion?

Both images were pleasurable enough to send a

roar of heat through his bloodstream. So strong that it took all his willpower not to reach out for her there and then.

'If we don't spend any time at all together Salvatore is going to start smelling a rat,' he lied. 'I already told him we had a date night.' He pushed away the memory of his grandfather's bewildered question, *Flora who?*

She gave a defeated sigh. 'Oh, all right, then.' She got to her feet at the same time as him. 'But I need my bag.'

He stood waiting, the display of foot-tapping a bit over the top considering it had taken her barely five minutes to pick up her bag and a light wrap and swop her flat ballet pumps for a pair of sandals with heels.

'I looked in on Jamie,' she said, hating that she felt the need to justify herself as she panted to keep up with the long-legged pace he set as he led her out into the courtyard and over to a long, low-slung, power-statement convertible.

'This is yours, I think.' She held out her hand.

He looked at the cufflink but there was nothing to read in his expression. 'Thanks. I stopped by last night to look in on the baby. You were asleep.'

She wanted to ask him if she'd only dreamt being in his arms, dreamt his heartbeat, but she couldn't risk the answer being yes, and looking like a total idiot who dreamt of him—even if it was a fairly accurate assessment.

The top of the car was down as they drove down

the winding road from the Castello to the small town beside the sea.

It seemed to Flora that the farther they got from the Castello, the more relaxed Ivo became. The tension left his shoulders, even the lines bracketing his mouth relaxed.

His next comment confirmed her observation.

'That place...' He glanced at the reflection in the rear-view mirror. 'It's oppressive.'

It seemed a strange way for anyone to speak about their home. 'It's very beautiful, but if somewhere has bad associations, I suppose—'

'My father killed himself in his flat in Rome, if that is what you mean by bad associations, and I do not live in the past.' He was living in the present. The problem was the present was not a very uplifting place to be; witnessing the disintegration of his grandfather was agonising. 'I simply have no taste for living in a museum.'

The drive had taken only minutes. They were already passing under a massive stone arch and into the town, at which point the feeling of freedom and wind in her hair vanished. They slowed to a snail's pace.

'They've pedestrianised the old town, which is good, but it's kind of moved the problem out here,' Ivo explained above the cacophony of car horns.

This part looked pretty old to Flora. He slammed on the brakes and threw out a curse as a scooter cut across them. The driver looked back and grinned.

'I'll park here and we'll walk in. It's only a few minutes, even in those heels.'

'I didn't think you'd noticed.'

'I was meant to, then?'

She slung him a look and he chuckled softly as he turned off the road and pulled the car onto a cobbled area and went round to open the passenger door for her. She managed a graceful exit, even though he was looking at her legs.

'Yes, very good shoes.'

Flora made a snorting sound.

'It's this way. I think you'll like it. It's right on the water and the seafood is excellent.'

They walked down the cobbled streets that became narrower as they got nearer the waterfront. The place was buzzing with a mixture of holidaymakers and locals, the atmosphere relaxed, almost festive.

'This is really lovely but are you sure us…this…? It wasn't part of our arrangement. Things are getting a bit, well, blurred.' She gnawed nervously on her lower lip, gave an awkward little grimace and lifted her eyes with appeal to his. 'Don't you think?'

'Are you regretting sleeping with me?'

Her eyes flew wide. 'No, of course not.'

'Then I don't see a problem.'

He stood aside and let her enter the restaurant ahead of him, then as he joined her he placed his hand lightly in the small of her back.

The restaurant owner appeared almost immediately, greeting Ivo by name.

Ivo in turn introduced Flora, then the man personally led them past the diners inside to a table beside the water.

A romantic spot, or it would have been but for the tables joined together to accommodate a large family group who were having a celebratory dinner.

The manager said something to Ivo, who translated for her benefit.

'It's the grandmother's eightieth birthday. He asked if you'd prefer a quieter spot?'

'I'm fine...if you are?'

'You all right with the noise?' Ivo asked as the table began to clap the arrival of a large birthday cake laden with candles.

Before she could assure him she was fine, that she loved the atmosphere of the place, a toy car landed in the dish of olives in the centre of the table, splashing Ivo with oil.

She didn't know what she expected his reaction to be but laughter wasn't it. One of the adults at the table had got to his feet but Ivo was quicker. He picked the car up and, wiping it on a napkin, he walked across to the table.

She watched, her expression growing wistful as he handed it to a toddler in a high chair and said something to the adults that sent up a roar of laughter. He was so good with children.

It was no struggle to see him with his own one day, a brood to carry on his family name and a wife he could be proud of.

For some reason she felt her eyes fill.

Some reason? Really, Flora, who are you kidding?

Her heart ached because she would never be that woman, but Ivo was born to be a father.

'You want to move?' he asked softly when he returned to the table and retook his place.

Flora blinked hard. 'No, I'm fine, unless you—'

She was interrupted by a loud shout from a man across the restaurant. 'Little brat! This is a disgrace! Hey, don't you people know how to control your kids? People are here to escape their kids... Never heard of a babysitter, mate? You... Hey, you... I want to see the manager! Don't you know who I am?'

She could see the look of contempt on Ivo's face and was sure that it was an expression mirrored around the place.

'I'm sorry about this,' Ivo murmured.

'What have you to be sorry about?' she asked. 'Anyway, he's a Brit—maybe *I* should be the one apologising. I think he's trying to impress his lady friend. You know, he reminds me of someone I used to know,' she confided, lowering her voice to a confidential murmur.

'Who?'

She gave a shame-faced grimace. 'Callum. He always liked to be the centre of attention, too.'

Ivo didn't seek attention but he commanded it. She felt a stab of disbelief when she remembered comparing the two men in her head.

She must have been blind!

Her eyes went to the strong, beautiful man sitting across from her and the idea of falling in love with someone you had only known for a matter of days no longer seemed something to laugh at.

It was no joke.

It was real.

It was a fact.

She felt weirdly light-headed as she embraced the sense of relief, along with the pain she'd been avoiding.

She suddenly felt more alive than she had done in an age. She had so much to give, she knew that— the sadness was he didn't want to take, not her heart anyway. But she'd give him what he did want, which, for the moment at least, was her body.

Afterwards, she'd deal with the hurt.

Her glance lifted from the glass of wine she was clutching to where Ivo sat across the table. She wanted to say, Let's leave. Take me to bed, love me.

She was framing the bold words in her head but when she saw his face, her resolve faltered and faded.

The contempt she'd seen stamped into the aristo-cratic angles and planes was still there but the over-whelming impression now, as he looked past her and into the main dining area, was chilling hauteur that, as she watched, tipped over into anger as the tipsy tourist launched into the second act of his ti-rade, his voice drowning out the clearly pacifying responses of the manager, who was attempting to calm the situation.

One of the children at the table started crying and

Ivo, mouth compressed, eyes like ice, put his glass down and glanced over at Flora.

'If you'll excuse me, this won't take a moment.'

'No!' Without thinking she reached across the table and grabbed his sleeve. 'Don't go, please, leave it. Let someone else.' Of course, she knew that Ivo wasn't the person who *let someone else.*

He *was* the someone else.

He smiled into her worried face. 'It's fine. I'm not going to ask him to step outside.' Unless absolutely necessary.

She watched as Ivo approached the table, somehow managing to look urbane and darkly menacing at the same time.

She couldn't hear what he said to make the tourist go quiet but whatever it was didn't stop the wife taking a selfie of herself with Ivo.

Ivo received several nods of approving gratitude as he walked back to the table.

Leaning down, he caught Flora's hand, brought it up to his lips. She was caught unawares; the tingle from the contact went all the way down to her curling toes. The hypnotic tug of his dark eyes was utterly irresistible, and she sat transfixed by a wave of lustful sheer longing.

'What did you say to him?'

'I told him we were newly engaged and were enjoying a private dinner. A private, *quiet* dinner.'

Their glances connected. The pupils of his dark eyes had expanded dramatically, and she could hear his laboured breaths—or were they her own?

Flora felt the well of love inside her expand until she could barely breathe; the noise of the rest of the room faded out.

It was Ivo who broke the spell.

'Let's get out of here,' he growled.

She didn't say anything, she couldn't; she just nodded.

They both stood up. Ivo peeled notes from a money clip in his pocket and laid them on the table, grabbed her hand and together they walked out.

'You paid and we didn't eat.' She realised as they reached the car.

His dark eyes flickered her way. 'You want to go back?'

'No, I want you to make love to me.'

Without a word he walked around the car to her side, put one hand behind her head; the other he curved over her bottom and pulled her tight into his body, sealing them at hip level before he covered her mouth with his.

When he lifted his head, he pinned her with a stare like hot smoke. 'That's what I want too. I hope you noticed.'

She gulped. 'I noticed.'

'I should go.' Head pressed into the pillow, one hand curved above her head, she studied the dark intense features of the man lying beside her. She reached out and touched the rough shadow on his jaw; there were places on her body that were red from the abrasive contact with the stubbly growth.

The first time they had literally fallen into one another, ripping off clothes in a frenzy of desire, the coupling had been equally raw and her climax, when it had come, so intense that she'd thought she'd faint.

Then later it had been much slower, slow and sensual. He had explored every inch of her body and encouraged reciprocation. Encouraged experimentation. Learning what pleased him had only increased her own pleasure.

'Go?'

The fingers moving in sweeping arabesques up the warm, still slightly damp skin of her back stopped for a moment, and then continued their nerve-tingling progress.

'Why?' he asked, lifting a skein of bright hair from her cheek so that he could see her face.

'Because you've already said you have an early flight and the doctor is dropping by first thing to see Jamie.' And hopefully pronounce him fighting fit.

'Stay a little longer...?'

She sighed—who could resist?—and curled into him, pressing a kiss to his stubble-roughened cheek. 'I really thought that the other diners were going to cheer you tonight.'

He gave a grunt and stroked her hair.

'What did you *really* say to him?'

'I don't remember.' His hand stilled. 'Did he hurt you, your ex?'

She lifted her head and raised herself up on one

elbow to look down at him. 'That was a bit out of the blue.'

'You said the loser in the restaurant reminded you of him...'

She settled back down, pressing her face into his chest. 'He dumped me because I can't have children. It seems he wanted a *real* woman.'

He responded to her little sigh with a low growl and flipped her over onto her back before settling over her. 'You are a very *real* woman...' Pinning her arms above her head with one hand, he curled a hand around the side of her face and kissed her hard and long, as if he could drain the pain from her.

She closed her eyes as he slid down, pressing his face into her neck as his body came to rest heavy and hot on her. She loved the musky smell of his warm, damp skin, the weight of him pushing into her. She wanted to hold onto the memory of this moment.

They lay there for a while, she wasn't sure how long, when she sensed the tension building in him.

'I would have come to the funeral, you know, but I didn't know. Not that Bruno was dead, not about Jamie. I would have known, if...'

Lying very still, hardly daring to breathe, Flora silently willed him to go on.

'Bruno reached out to me. He wanted to meet up. I think he wanted to tell me about the pregnancy, Jamie, but I refused.'

She felt a deep sigh shudder through his body.

'I was punishing him, you see, because when he

left he said he'd come back for me and he didn't, but it turns out he did.' His bitter laugh was muffled in her hair.

'You didn't know,' she soothed, aching for the pain she heard in his voice, the fact that he was beating himself up for something that wasn't his fault. 'I miss Bruno too, and Sami.' She felt the tears she couldn't stop seep out from her closed eyelids; after a moment, so did Ivo.

His arms slid around her as he pulled her onto her side so that they were lying facing one another. The sound of her sobs made him feel as though his heart were being dragged out of his chest. It was unbearable. He lay there holding her, feeling more helpless than he'd ever felt in his life and conscious that none of this felt like safe, meaningless sex.

The next time she said she should go to her own bed, he didn't object.

CHAPTER TWELVE

'So, HE IS FINE?'

The doctor smiled. 'The picture of health.'

'And his heart—has the virus caused any damage?'

'None whatsoever.'

'Sorry, I'm a bit paranoid.'

'Not at all, it's perfectly understandable.' He extended his hand. 'Well, I hope the next time we meet it will not be in a professional capacity. Good morning, Ms Henderson.'

The bang on the door came so soon after his departure that she assumed the doctor had forgotten something and returned.

In the middle of changing Jamie's nappy, she was about to call out when the door crashed in, loudly and violently enough to make her protective instincts kick in.

She grabbed the baby and rose to her feet with him clutched in her arms.

The downgrading of her alarm when she saw that it was Salvatore standing in the doorway was brief because this was a very different Salvatore from the benign, smiling, jolly figure from their breakfast earlier in the week. He actually looked generally dishevelled, unshaven; his silver hair didn't look as though it had seen a comb for some time.

'Good morning. Is there anything wrong?' she asked, noticing the splodges of something down his shirt front.

'Is it true?'

She shook her head, bemused not just by the question but by the aggressive way it was delivered.

'I'm sorry, I don't—'

'I've no time for this. I have meetings…*important* meeting to go to. Do you deny that you are barren?'

The brutality took her breath away. 'It's true that I can't have children.'

'And that this child has a defective heart?'

'Jamie has a minor heart defect, yes.'

'Grecos do not have defects. Grecos' hearts are strong. Grecos are strong!' he bellowed. 'I know what your game is… You can tell them I know…'

Close to tears by this point, she hugged Jamie close to her. 'I haven't got a game. There is no *them*.' She shrank back as the old man stamped towards them, stopping a few feet away, but close enough for her to see the spittle on his lips as he waved his fist at her.

'Ivo will give me strong heirs. If you marry him I will disinherit him.' Having delivered his parting threat, he turned and stomped away.

Flora's knees just folded under her and she sat down cross-legged on the floor with the baby clenched against her chest.

She had woken this morning feeling so much hope, so much optimism. Last night, in her head at least, had been a breakthrough. Ivo had actually shared something with her and she had confided her secret to him; he hadn't recoiled in horror... She scrunched her eyes tight shut and let out a low wail of anguish as she rocked with Jamie clutched to her chest.

No, he'd not recoiled, instead he'd gone straight to his grandfather and shared the intimate, private information! That hurt far more than the old man's ranting and cruelty. Maybe Ivo had gone seeking advice? How he could extricate himself from this barren creature? Oh, she was good enough for the odd tumble but she was getting ideas there might be more.

'And I was,' she told her waxen reflection in the mirror. 'I thought he might be growing to care for me...love me.' Back against the wall, she pushed herself to her feet, feeling old as she walked across to the mirror, pushing her face towards it as she sneered, 'You idiot... Flora, you stupid fool.'

Ivo was halfway to the airport when Ramon's voice-mail reached him.

'Sir, there has been an incident with your grand-father. I think you should get back now.'

* * *

'Sir!'

Ramon was waiting as he burst into the hallway.

'Your grandfather, he has confronted Ms Henderson, and I think—'

Ivo swore. 'Talk and walk.'

The older man did talk, though in a series of gasps as he struggled to keep pace with Ivo's long-legged stride.

By the time Ivo reached the door to the nursery wing there were some gaps but he knew enough not to be surprised when he walked in and found Flora, wearing a coat and stuffing baby clothes in a bag.

'What are you doing?'

She turned. The tear stains on her cheeks gave lie to her calm expression and the oddly emotionless delivery of her response.

'I'm going back home. Jamie's all better and I don't think we are very welcome any more.'

'I don't know what he's said—'

She held up a hand to stop him. 'No, I'm grateful really, your grandfather just explained things to me, things like how you need a *proper* woman with all the equipment in full working order. Oh, and he's not overly struck, it seems, on *defective* babies...'

'Flora—'

Ignoring his agonised cry, she held him off with an outstretched hand and a narrow-eyed stare of loathing before he'd taken more than a step towards her.

'Do *not* come near me!' she snapped. 'You know,

I actually think I hate you, you know that? I thought, I actually thought, that you c-cared!' She swallowed and bit down hard on her wobbling lower lip. 'How long was it before you rushed to tell him about my defectiveness? Oh, the ring, I almost forgot and I don't know why you were so worried—it's not as though we were really engaged so there's no chance he'll disinherit you.' She twisted it off her finger and flung it onto the top of a bureau.

'Disinherit?'

'Oh, did I miss out that bit? Well, you can tell him that there is no chance we are getting married, that there never was, so problem solved.' Just the little matter of living with regret and sticking together the pieces of her broken, disillusioned heart.

She stood there looking brittle and fragile and *hurting*, stood there looking at him as though he were a stranger, and Ivo wanted to rush over her and hold her.

If only he'd spoken last night when she would have listened, but he'd bottled it, he told himself in disgust, remembering the thing close to panic that had gripped him when he had realised the actual extent of his feelings for Flora. The *real* reason why he had felt her pain more keenly than his own.

If only he had not let her go last night.

If only he'd never hidden Salvatore's condition.

Well, you can speak now, so what are you waiting for?

'I won't tell him that.'

Her eyes flew wide. 'Why on earth not? You want me to put it in writing?'

'No, because it wouldn't be true.'

The tears quivering on her eyelashes, shining in her swimming cerulean eyes, snapped something inside him.

'Cara mia...!'

'Don't come near me, Ivo, just let me go,' she wailed.

'I'm not going to tell my grandfather anything because it is likely he has forgotten what he said to you.'

She pulled the baby vest she had absently blotted her tears on and stared at him. 'What do you mean, forgotten?'

'My grandfather has Alzheimer's disease, Flora. You know what that is?'

Her eyes flew wide in horrified comprehension.

'He has never been a nice or kind man, he is ruthless and a stranger to empathy, but he is my grandfather and once, when I was small and in a very bad place, he rescued me.'

'Your father...?'

He nodded. 'And now he is the one who is scared. He knows that he is slipping away and he can't do anything about it. He forgets, he remembers, he tries to hide it, but the paranoia, the conspiracy theories are a new development. He does not want people to know. He hates the idea of being an object of pity and I agreed. I see now, of course, that I should have warned you. As for the threats of disinheriting me, he gave me power of attorney, with just such an event as this in mind.' He glanced towards the baby. 'Jamie's inheritance is safe.'

'I am very sorry about your grandfather. I was really confused but it makes sense now. Is there anything I can say or do to make it easier for him? For you?'

'You are a really good person, Flora, you know that? The thing is he will have forgotten he said it by the next time you see him.'

She walked across to one of the cases and shut it.

He frowned at the symbolic gesture.

'I really don't think we should risk that, Ivo, do you?'

He growled out, 'You're not going!'

She went across and touched his arm. She could feel the quivering tension in the taut muscles through the fabric of his jacket. 'I would stay, I really would. I'm having the best time with you, but the thing is I need more than this half-love thing. I love you and you... Well, you don't love me. I'm not blaming you,' she added hastily when she saw his expression. 'I understand, and to be honest it's probably for the best given my...' Without her realising it, her free hand had gone to her stomach. 'You have so much to pass on, not just all this, but love—you should have children, Ivo, and I'm not going to deprive you of that.'

'Have you finished?'

She nodded.

'Good, because I have some things to say, too.

And for the record I always knew you couldn't have children. It was one of the things that Salvatore told me and then forgot and then presumably remembered in some twisted way. As for an heir, I already have one.' He took both of her small, cold hands in his and looked down at the baby kicking on the rug.

'I need a son, Jamie needs a father. It is my intention to adopt him after we are married.'

'I love Jamie,' she choked out, 'but I'm not marrying you for him.'

'I am not asking you to. I'm asking you for me.' He pulled her captured hands up to his chest and pressed them over his heart so that she could feel the echo of his life force thudding beneath her fingertips.

She looked into his eyes and for a moment she forgot how to breathe because the love shining down at her was so all-consuming.

Could this really be happening?

'I have spent my life seeing love as a weakness to be guarded against. I told myself that I was the strong one and others were fools.' His mouth twisted in a grimace of self-contempt. 'I was the fool, not strong, but weak and scared. You have taught me that, and there is more you can teach me, I'm sure. Meeting you has changed my life. It's set me free. I'm not offering you a half-life or half-love, *cara*, I'm offering you complete love. My whole heart.'

By the time he had finished the tears were streaming unchecked down Flora's cheeks.

'I love you, Ivo, with all my heart I love you.'

He smiled a slow smile that made her heart flip. 'You'll marry me.'

'When?'

'Tomorrow.' They'd done everything so far in a short period of time and he didn't see any reason to stop now.

'That would not be a good first impression to make on your mother-in-law.'

'A compromise…a week?'

'A month.'

Eyes dancing, he nodded. 'Deal.'

She held out her hand. 'Should we shake on it?'

Grinning, he grabbed her arm and jerked her towards him. 'Kiss on it.'

With a deep sigh Flora fell into his embrace.

EPILOGUE

FLORA HAD BEEN dozing when the door opened.

'Hello, there.' She smiled and pulled herself upright as Jamie entered the room, his dark hair slicked back, his shoes freshly shined, a posy of flowers clutched in one chubby hand, the other enfolded in the hand of the man who walked in beside him.

'You've come to see your new baby sister?'

Jamie shook his head, though his eyes kept swivelling to the cot at the side of the bed.

'No, I've come to see you, Mama, because you're my favourite person and I have to make a fuss of you or you might get jealous.'

Flora's laughing eyes turned to her husband. 'Thank you, darling, you are my favourite person too.'

'I know,' the little boy said smugly. He crept in closer and, lifting his hand to his face, lowered his voice. 'But we won't tell her,' he whispered. He glanced back towards the tall figure behind him. 'It wouldn't be kind, and I will always be kind to my little sister. Is she nice?'

'I think she might be. Now, tell me about your day and then if you like you can hold your sister.'

'My day was good, I helped Nanny Emily pick up toys 'cos she's incredibly old—maybe even thirty?' He glanced to Ivo for conformation and received a solemn nod in return. 'I thought so, and Nana Grace told me the story about how my mummy Sami once fell in the sea with all her clothes on…*cold* sea…and when she was born she had golden curls. Does Samantha have curls?' He edged his way towards the cot.

'She does.' Flora, a lump of emotion in her throat, glanced towards Ivo, who smiled back at her with his eyes. It was amazing but she knew he was remembering, as she was, the moment their miracle baby had put in her appearance.

She lifted a hand to her own head. 'But I'm afraid they are like mine. See for yourself.'

Ivo lifted Jamie up so the boy could get a better look at the sleeping baby. 'So, what do you think?'

'She's cool…but a bit small.'

Ivo looked over their son's head at his sleeping daughter who, for the first four months after her conception, Flora had been convinced was a *grumbling appendix*, or else something too bad to put a name to.

He had gone with her when she had booked herself a doctor's appointment, prepared for the worst and determined to be strong for his wife of two years.

The first clue they'd had was when the doctor had asked if they'd been trying for a baby.

Flora had told him that she wasn't able to have

children and then he'd dropped his bombshell. It had taken the scan to convince her, the image of the tiny life inside her on the screen.

They'd left the office shell-shocked.

Ivo liked to think that his grandfather had understood when they'd told him they were having a baby, but it was hard to tell as by that point Salvatore had needed twenty-four-hour, round-the-clock care.

He had passed away in his sleep a week later.

But there was a permanent monument to his memory: they had just completed the transfer of the Castello and its contents to charity, which was going to open it to the public as a museum.

They had moved to a sprawling farmhouse in the hills more suited to a family home. His clever wife had overseen the entire renovation and designed the massive modern extension with the glass walls that looked out over olive groves and the Tuscan hills.

'Can I wake her up?'

'Ivo!' Flora exclaimed. 'I'm going to remind you of that in two weeks' time when you're walking around like a sleep-deprived zombie. You'll be longing for the days of peace and quiet.'

'I've had enough quiet in my life, enough of being alone. I like my life noisy and messy and filled with my family.'

It sounded like a winning formula to Flora, who was too happy to protest when he scooped his baby daughter out of the crib.

* * * * *

COMING NEXT MONTH FROM

H HARLEQUIN

Presents.

Available March 19, 2019

#3705 THE ITALIAN DEMANDS HIS HEIRS
Billionaires at the Altar
by Lynne Graham
To counter a media scandal, Raffaele must marry Vivi. And he's not above using seduction to convince her! But when Vivi discovers she's pregnant, Raffaele demands she meet him down the aisle—for real!

#3706 THE SICILIAN'S SECRET SON
Secret Heirs of Billionaires
by Angela Bissell
When Luca uncovers the existence of his hidden son, he's determined to whisk his new family away to his Sicilian estate. But Luca knows there's only one way to truly claim Annah and his son—marriage!

#3707 INNOCENT'S NINE-MONTH SCANDAL
One Night With Consequences
by Dani Collins
When Rozalia appears on Viktor's doorstep, his world is thrown into chaos! But their passion has consequences...and Viktor refuses to let scandal ruin his family. Their baby will be legitimate! And Rozi? She will be his...

#3708 CHOSEN AS THE SHEIKH'S ROYAL BRIDE
Conveniently Wed!
by Jennie Lucas
Beth can hardly believe Sheikh Omar would even notice her. So when she's chosen as his bride, she's stunned. Thrown into a world of unimagined luxury, can this shy Cinderella ever be a queen?

HPCNM0319RA

#3709 SPANIARD'S BABY OF REVENGE
by Clare Connelly

Antonio plans to persuade innocent Amelia to sell her shares in his rival's business. But he doesn't plan on their intense connection—and is stunned to discover their nine-month consequence. To secure his child, he'll make Amelia his wife!

#3710 CLAIMING MY UNTOUCHED MISTRESS
by Heidi Rice

Edie agreed to clear her family's debts by posing as my temporary mistress, helping expose my business rivals. Yet Edie's innocence is a temptation I couldn't have imagined. Our chemistry is spectacular—now I'll claim Edie for more than pleasure!

#3711 REUNITED BY A SHOCK PREGNANCY
by Chantelle Shaw

Sienna should not be secretly attending her ex-husband's wedding. Until she realizes Nico isn't the groom... But when he follows her, their burning fire reignites, leaving Sienna shockingly pregnant with the Italian's child!

#3712 THE BILLIONAIRE'S VIRGIN TEMPTATION
by Michelle Conder

Ruby is stunned when Sam sweeps her into an anonymous seduction! But when Ruby realizes Sam is her new boss, and they're left stranded together, his forbidden touch could be powerful enough to unravel Ruby forever...

YOU CAN FIND MORE INFORMATION ON UPCOMING HARLEQUIN® TITLES, FREE EXCERPTS AND MORE AT WWW.HARLEQUIN.COM.

HPCNM0319RB

Get 4 FREE REWARDS!

We'll send you 2 FREE Books plus 2 FREE Mystery Gifts.

Harlequin Presents® books feature a sensational and sophisticated world of international romance where sinfully tempting heroes ignite passion.

FREE Value Over **$20**

*Walking into my casino, Edie Spencer seemed like a
spoiled heiress—until she agreed to clear her family's
debts by posing as my temporary mistress. My plan? To
use her to expose my business rivals. Yet discovering
Edie's innocence has led to greater temptation than I
could have imagined. Our chemistry is spectacular—
now I'll claim Edie for so much more than pleasure!*

*Read on for a sneak preview of
Heidi Rice's next story,*
Claiming My Untouched Mistress.

"Your sister told me exactly how deep your financial troubles go,"
I said. "I have a possible solution."

"What is it?" Edie said, desperation plain on her face.

"Would you consider working for me?" I asked.

"You're…you're offering me a job?"

She sounded so surprised, I found my lips curving in amusement
again.

"As it happens, I am hosting an event at my new estate near
Nice at the end of the month. I could use your skills as part of the
team I'm putting together."

"What exactly do you need me to do?" she said, her eagerness
a sop to my ego.

"The guests I am inviting are some of the world's most powerful
businessmen and women." I outlined the job. "They have all shown
an interest in investing in the expansion of the Allegri brand. The
event is a way of assessing their suitability as investors. As part of
the week, I will be offering some recreational poker events. These

HPEXP0319

people are highly competitive and they enjoy games of chance. What they don't know is that how they play poker tells me a great deal more about their personalities and their business acumen— and whether we will be compatible—than a simple profit-and-loss portfolio of their companies. But I find that successful people, no matter how competitive they are, are also smart enough to know that they cannot best me at a poker table. So I need someone who does not intimidate them, but who can observe how they play and make those assessments for me." I kept my eyes on her reaction, surprised myself by how much I wanted her to say yes.

My attraction to her might be unexpected, but I had spent a lifetime living by my wits and never doubting my instincts. When I had originally considered giving her a hosting position I'd been aware of the possible fringe benefits for both of us and I didn't see why that should change. She had made it very clear she was more than happy to blur the lines between employer and lover, and all her responses made it equally clear she desired me as much as I desired her.

"I'll pay you four thousand euros for the fortnight," I said, to make her position clear. This was a genuine job, and a job she would be very good at. "Joe can brief you on each of the participants— and what I need to know about them. If you do a good enough job, and your skills prove as useful as I'm expecting them to be, I would consider offering you a probationary position."

She blinked several times, her skin now flushed a dark pink, but didn't say anything.

"So do you want the job?" I asked, letting my impatience show, annoyed by the strange feeling of anticipation. Why should it matter to me if she declined my offer?

"Yes, yes," she said. "I'll take the job."

Don't miss
Claiming My Untouched Mistress.
Available April 2019 wherever
Harlequin® Presents books and ebooks are sold.

www.Harlequin.com